Municipal Blondes

Other Titles
by Nathan Everett

City Limits

GEE EVARS WANDERED into Rosebud Falls on Independence Day just in time to rescue a toddler from the rushing torrent of the Rose River. And to lose his memory. In an attempt to make Rosebud Falls his home, Gee becomes a local hero and inadvertently leads a revolt that changes the balance of power in the town. But will he ever know who he really is?

Wild Woods

LED BY CITY Champion Gee Evars, the man without a memory, Rosebud Falls has annexed the Wild Woods and torn down the fence separating it from the Forest. But the Wild Woods holds its own mysteries, including the key to drug dealing, child trafficking, and Gee's own unknown history. Long-awaited change comes to the Families of Rosebud Falls.

For Money or Mayhem

COMPUTER FORENSICS DETECTIVE Dag Hamar is pulled from behind the safety of his computer and takes to the streets when he discovers a link between an online predator and real life kidnappings around Seattle. His fledgling romance is threatened when his girlfriend's daughter is suddenly among the missing.

For Blood or Money

COMPUTER FORENSICS DETECTIVES Dag Hamar and Deb Riley discover secret files and hidden code can be as dangerous as dark alleys and flying bullets as they track a missing man and the billion-dollar fortune that went with him. Fourteen years after *For Money or Mayhem*.

Read Excerpts at http://www.NathanEverett.com

Municipal Blondes

Nathan Everett

ELDER ROAD BOOKS
BELLEVUE WA

{ Contents }

Municipal Blondes

{1}
He hit me, humiliated me, and shot me

I'M GLAD THE SON OF A BITCH is dead! And no one will tell me how Dag is, or where he is. *Damn it!* This is as bad as being held hostage by those bastards in the first place.

Whine and cry.

———+ + + + + +IIIII+ + + + + +———

Recovery

I'M SITTING—OR LYING—IN a hospital bed in Seattle with my right side bandaged up and antibiotics pumping into me. I've got a towel wrapped around my head because the fucker knocked my wig off when he slugged me. It's going to cost a bundle to get that one replaced. I can't talk because my jaw is so sore and my lip and eye are all swollen up. My head hurts and they have something dripping into my arm that makes my thinking fuzzy but doesn't seem to stop the pain.

I want Dag!

He came to save me. He knocked out Angel's ex-Marine boyfriend and tied him up. He got Oksamma out of the apartment and locked him on the roof. He attacked Bradley with some kind of kitchen poker or something and was nearly killed when Bradley shot. If he hadn't handed me a knife when he went after Bradley, I'd never have gotten loose in time to trip up Oksamma and get him in the way of the bullet. That ruined my silk scarf, too.

The glass was still falling out of the window when I grabbed Dag and dragged him to the elevator. We fell into the car and the door was closing when Oksamma managed to get off a lucky shot that tore through the skin on the side of my right breast. It didn't hit anything vital but it ripped the hell out of my side and they put God-knows-how-many stitches in it.

I passed out and Dag carried me out of the building. In his condition! Jordan pulled up and fired a life-saving shot before the car came to a rest. Dag pushed me into his arms and fell.

There were policemen and ambulances and Jordan rode to the hospital with me in the second ambulance. The first ambulance was full of people trying to keep Dag alive. I was lying there and Jordan was holding a pad on my side to staunch the flow of blood. When he looked at me, I realized I didn't have a wig on. I was mortified. But Jordan just stroked my head once and said, "Nice do, Deb. I like it." He gave me a towel and helped me wrap my head before we got to the hospital. He never even flinched away from me.

But when he came up to see me an hour ago, he still didn't have any word on Dag. He thought he was in ICU. If I can get disconnected from these pipes and hoses, I'm going looking for him myself.

God! What a day! What a night last night. I'm glad Jordan shot Oksamma. I'm glad Bradley Keane is dead. It would make me happy to find out Brenda Barnett was gone, too. I guess you can't ask for everything.

I just want to curl up in bed at home and cry. Why won't anyone tell me where Dag is?

I kissed him

It wasn't even much of a romantic kiss. I just saw him lying in that bed and leaned over and kissed him. And he woke up.

Stevie brought me a wig this morning and Teri brought me clothes. My little black dress is like ruined. The hospital discharged me and I ran to the office. I called Mrs. Prior yesterday to tell her Dag was in the hospital and make sure she had Maizie. I wanted to check the office. Dag really left it a mess. The vault was standing open and his laptop was on the desk. Bubble wrap and tape were on the floor. He must have been so angry when Bradley called him.

I tidied up and made sure the backup disks I'd stolen from Brenda's house were in the vault. I closed it securely. Grabbing Dag's laptop, I headed back to the hospital. At least they told me where he was and let me sit in his room with him. I sat there all afternoon fiddling with the computer until I looked up at him and I just had to kiss him.

Not much of a kiss. He's got tubes in his nose for oxygen and a heart monitor hooked up to him. His lips were dry and mine are—let's just say puffy and leave it at that. But when I kissed him, he woke up.

I was so afraid I would never get to speak to him again.

They have him prepped for heart transplant but there's no donor. I'd give him mine.

I don't know why they even allowed me in the room but I think it has to do with something Jordan told them. They treat me like I'm his next of kin. The doctor even told me that he was checking on Dag regularly and I should call for him if there was any change.

Dag and I didn't talk for long when he woke up. He's so weak. But at least he knew I kissed him. And he stroked my cheek. If I touch it myself, the pain is so intense that I flinch but his fingers were so soft and gentle that it didn't hurt at all.

I'm writing a lot of foolish emo. I just... After yesterday... Everyone seems so fragile. I'm not going home tonight. I want to be here when he wakes up again.

———————————————

The mountain came out

As you may have heard on national news, Seattle and surrounds got hit with a major blizzard last night. Everything is pretty much closed down. People on 405 were stranded all night in their cars. People abandoned their cars on the bridge and walked. Today it didn't get above freezing but the sun came out and it was bright and sunny. This afternoon, I was standing by the window in Dag's hospital room and realized I was looking at Mount

Rainier. It was glorious.

I went to the nurses' station and begged them to help me move Dag's bed so he could see out the window. He's wanted to look at the mountain all month. He just stands by his window at the office or in his apartment. Dr. Roberts intervened and even helped move the bed. There it was in all its glory with the setting sun glinting off its glaciers. I cranked his bed up to a sitting position so he could see out the window. He took my hand as we stared out the window.

"I climbed it once," he said in a faraway voice. "It's not the top of the world, but it's one of the upper floors. You should see the view. It was clear and sunny and you could see Olympus, Baker, Adams, St. Helens. If you ever get the chance, girl, climb that mountain. You won't be the same person when you come down."

"You can show me," I answered. "Maybe next summer."

"We'll have to train. Might have to be the summer after. You don't go climbing that old man without training," he said. "Yes. We'll do it summer after. That should give us time."

———— +‒+‒+‒++HⅢH++‒+‒+ ————

THE MOUNTAIN MUST have revitalized him. He was amazing. He totally figured out the scheme and nailed the Muffin-Top. Jordan arrested her on the spot. I had no idea that BKL was her initials as well as the name of the company. I wouldn't have put it together if I'd known. He was so sharp. I know it hurt a little. He loved her once and thought she was his life mate. I can't see it now but, like Dag says, people change.

Then in the afternoon he was so far away. When he sent me to the bank, I went home and changed clothes. It took forever to get around because all the buses are on their snow routes and they don't even do my hill. I put on the suit that's always been his favorite. He doesn't say much about what I wear, other than the day I came to the office in blue jeans.

"Riley," he said, "if I'd hired you to work on a farm, I'd expect you to dress like a farmer. This is an office."

He's always complimentary about my professional clothes, though, and I notice him looking at me a lot when I wear this particular suit. It's pretty plain—just a dark blue-gray skirt and blazer. Well, the skirt might be a little short for most offices but I like to tease him. I wear it with a cream silk blouse that plunges forever. It looks fine as long as I don't take my jacket off. Then, watch out! The strand of pearls my father gave me for my sixteenth birthday. Sixteen inches long.

I put on the more formal blonde wig that I wear when I'm going out. It's an updo and I save it for special occasions most of the time. I don't know why, but I wanted to look my very best and sexiest for him today.

As sexy as a girl with a fat lip and a black eye can look.

I swung by his apartment and picked up clean clothes for him and checked on Maizie. His coat and hat were at the office. He took off for the Condo Sunday and left them there. I picked them up and thought he'd be pleased that I brought fresh clothes for him. The suit he'd been wearing was in the hospital closet covered with blood. My blood.

I stood in the doorway and he just looked at me. If you've never had someone drink you in, this is an experience you want to have. You'll know what it's like to have been drunk! He motioned me over and looked at what I'd brought him.

"Oh good," he said. "You brought the gray one."

I stuttered a little. He didn't say anything about me. All his suits were gray.

"I'm joking, Riley," he said. "You have to learn a Swedish sense of humor." I'm such a dork! I can never tell when he's joking like that and I always get caught thinking he's serious. I showed him the lavender shirt and matching tie I got at Nordstrom on the way back. "Does this blue go with a gray suit?" he asked.

"Trust me," I answered. "You'll look stunning."

After he ate what meagre allotment of food he was allowed (all liquids, just in case a heart arrives in the middle of the night), we sat and talked and talked. I can't even tell you all the things we said. He told me about his high school sweetheart and what happened when he and Brenda were married. He told me about the summer he bought his Mustang and how he met Jordan. He even told me he'd planned to get married and lost his fiancée in a fire a few years ago. It was like he just wanted a few things from his life to be remembered.

My eyes are all watery and I can't see the keyboard. *Damn.*

He's asleep now. I can't stand it. I hate seeing him like this. I want to be held by him and told it will all be okay.

I love him.

{2}
It takes a thief

D AG NEEDS INFORMATION. That amazing brain of his put together a puzzle. Angel and Simon had tattoos with part of the security key. Dag says Bradley Keane had the missing set of numbers. He asked me to go find Bradley's body and copy down the characters on the tattoo.

I can't handle the truth of why I went on this foolish errand tonight. Dag asked me to. That's all I can handle and by God, I'm determined to do what he asked.

Term life insurance

I LEFT THE hospital and went to the office. An hour later, I found myself standing at the window staring out at the ferries and traffic like Dag did. When I realized what I was doing, my eyes were leaking. They've been doing that a lot lately. Ever since Sunday.

I started making calls. The city morgue was no help. No, they didn't have any record of Bradley Keane. I called the hospital where Dag is and they said they could only give information to next of kin. I wondered who that could be.

Funny.

I've examined a ton of Bradley's dirty little plans over the past month. I picked through his email. I looked at his bank accounts. I tracked his travel with Brenda. But I haven't really found out much about Bradley. I wondered who his next of kin was.

I started with a quick online search and the first thing that popped up was the newspaper story that ran on Tuesday. It was a small article in the back of the paper saying that Federal agents had broken a software counterfeiting ring on Sunday. Two suspects were killed. One was Bradley Keane, 49, who was a partner in the firm Barnett, Keane, and Lamb Ltd. Senior partner Simon Barnett was reported missing and presumed dead a week ago when his plane crashed in the Caribbean. Keane is survived by his widow, Sarah Keane and two children.

Whoa! Bradley was married? He was fooling around with Muffin-Top and he was married with children, too? This guy was too disgusting for words. I did a search and was rewarded with a home phone and address, compliments of the big name in telephones out here. Then I had to determine what I would do. I didn't have Simon's laptop anymore but I scanned through the old one Oksamma brought in when he cased our office. An insurance policy on all executives. Perfect. I would become an insurance adjuster and pay a little visit to Mrs. Keane.

People who pretend to be other people have it a lot easier now than a few years ago. I surprised Lars once after handing him a business card for a bank that no longer exists. He hadn't seen through my disguise as a banker. A quick search of the Internet this afternoon got me a logo for the American Insurance Company. I grabbed a photo from my private store of headshots in a conservative brunette wig, used one of my aliases, and had a professional glossy business card printing out of my inkjet in a matter of fifteen minutes.

I needed my car and that was a challenge. Sunday, I'd left it in the Condo parking garage. It was all I could do to steel myself to go back into that building. I know the Condo itself is sealed off and there isn't any danger now that Bradley and Oksamma are dead and Brenda's in jail, but still… It was hard to walk in there and just get in my car and drive out of the garage. And it cost me like a hundred bucks that I had to put on my credit card.

I got home okay and changed clothes into a nice conservative suit and my brunette wig. I was instantly Paula Winslow, insurance adjuster. I headed for the address in West Seattle where Bradley lived. Now, how much should the policy be for? Half a million? That sounded about right.

When I reached the house, I had to brace myself again. I clutched my folio in my hand and headed to the door, hoping my makeup was sufficient to hide the bruises on my face.

"Mrs. Keane?" I said when a matronly woman of about 50 opened the door. "I'm Paula Winslow of American Insurance Company. I don't want to disturb you but I was handling a matter in West Seattle and thought perhaps I could speed things up and spread a little comfort on this dreary afternoon. Is it convenient to talk with you for a few minutes?"

She looked me up and down like she was going to cut me a new suit. But she opened the door and let me in. She hadn't said anything but hello and I was a little spooked by the way she just turned and walked away. She motioned to a chair and sat on the sofa in the living room.

"I suppose you've come about Bradley," she said at last. I was beginning to feel like a schmuck.

"Yes," I said, plowing on. "Since I was near, I thought I might get a couple of details from you to help expedite the insurance payout. First, let me tell you how sorry I am to hear about your husband. It must be terribly hard on you."

"Thank you," she said, still watching me intently. I pulled out a yellow legal pad and started writing.

"The report we have indicates the time of death as shortly before noon on Sunday. Is that correct?"

"That's what they tell me."

"And what was the cause of death?"

"He fell through a window and was pierced by a piece of glass. That's the word the coroner used. Pierced, like it was for earrings." I had a vivid image in my mind of Oksamma crashing into Bradley and through the window. I wouldn't have used the word 'pierced.'

"So, the coroner did do an autopsy?" I asked.

"Yes. There was a rush because my husband was an organ donor. They called me and I signed the papers. I understand they harvested several organs for transplant. But because it was ruled an accidental death, there was no need to hold the body," she said. Perhaps even Bradley's worthless life could be redeemed by the pieces of his body transplanted into others.

"Does that mean they've released it to you for burial?" I asked. "Are you planning a memorial service?"

"A small one on Friday. They've taken him to Johnson & Sons Funeral Home. I have a card if you need it." *Bingo!* I accepted the card she picked up from the coffee table. I was surprised the house in West Seattle was no more ostentatious, like Simon and Brenda's house. You'd have to say it was pretty modest for a family of four. With the kind of money Bradley handled daily, this wasn't much in the way of digs.

"Well, if the coroner has ruled it an accidental death, there should be nothing to hold up payment of the death benefits on our end. I'll stop by the courthouse tomorrow and pick up a death certificate on my way to the office. I'm sure the extra cash will help keep bills met during this difficult time for you."

"Thank you." Again, a quiet, almost knowing stare at me. I realized she was looking at my swollen face. It was time to get out of there.

"I won't disturb your afternoon any further, Mrs. Keane," I said. "I trust you have everything you need at the moment. There is a storm approaching and the radio warned everyone to stay at home tonight." I stood and made my way to the door. Speaking of a storm, the temperature had dropped five or ten degrees just since I'd been inside and I was not wearing a heavy coat. I made it almost to the door when she stopped me short.

"I'm sorry about your face, Miss Riley," she said in that same quiet tone. I was on the defensive immediately, spinning to face her in case she attacked. She was still looking at me with the same intent stare. She continued, "I managed to get the whole story from the police. I know you were being held at that awful place he kept. I'm sorry. I understand your need to see the body and confirm it. But he's dead, Miss Riley. For all his faults, he was a good husband and father. If you can, let him rest."

"I..." She fluttered a hand at me breaking off what I was struggling to say and then walked away. I beat a hasty retreat back to my car. I wondered if it had been Jordan who came to tell her that her husband was dead. She was spooky.

———+++++++||||||||++++++—————

Once before I die

GETTING INTO THE funeral home was going to be another tricky task.

Our weather here has been freaky of late and the radio repeated the severe weather bulletin, encouraging people to go home early and batten down for Winter Storm Harper. Freezing rain and snow coated my windshield by the time I got to the funeral home. It was closed. I didn't want to try an unauthorized entry while people were around who could see me, so I went into a grocery store with a restaurant attached and sat to eat soup while I watched the weather close in off the Sound. I keep a change of clothes in the car in case I'm stranded and need to walk someplace in cold or rainy weather. I decided I'd better change.

It was after eight by the time I felt it was safe to break and enter. I'd watched the place for over an hour and had seen no sign that anyone was inside. At least no one alive. I left my car in the grocery store parking lot and headed for the back of the mortuary. I saw the alarm system wires just before I got the door open. It was an antiquated system. A quick snip with a nail clipper cut the alarm off. After all, how many people are going to break into a funeral home?

It didn't take long to find the refrigerator where Bradley was being kept. He'd already been dressed in a suit and placed in a coffin. That was going to make my job harder. I swore at the efficiencies of the coroner, the embalmer, and the aesthetician. The job would have been a lot easier if he'd been naked on a slab instead of fully dressed. He looked all too ready to sit up and defend himself. I sat across the room from him and shook for a long time. I wasn't sure I could go through with this.

I'm not going to tell you in detail what happened. I found a pair of rubber gloves. The rest is too gross to relive. I'll just say I found the tattoo. It was on his shoulder. A wreath with a banner woven across it. The letters were in the banner.

1SB41D1E.

I got him dressed again and put back in cold storage. I managed to get outside before I threw up. I was shaking so badly, I could hardly walk to the car. Driving was a nightmare. The streets were slippery and I had to drive slowly across the West Seattle Bridge and up to Capitol Hill. When I finally got back to my apartment, I was sick again and threw up in the toilet. I got in the shower and let the water run over me for an hour while I cried.

{3}
Nightmare

I HAD HAIR. Lots of hair. Long beautiful blond locks like Angel's. And I had hair under my arms. I couldn't even imagine shaving. And hair on my legs. And on my pubes. I couldn't help but run my fingers through it. I wanted to spend all day brushing it and shaking it back and forth like a wild animal. Long beautiful hair and it was all mine.

Dreaming

BUT I COULDN'T reach my hair. My hands were tied behind my back. I was sitting naked on a straight chair and Bradley was mocking me. He reached out and jerked out a big fistful of my hair. I thought he would tear my scalp apart when he pulled it. Then he jerked out another fistful. And another. Oksamma walked up beside him and hit me. Hair fell off my head with the jolt as if it were a wig. He hit me again. And again.

They were ripping out all my beautiful hair and my mother was laughing. I could hear her yelling, "Hey Baldy!" and smelled alcohol on her breath. I had just one lock of hair left on my head. Everything else was bald. He reached out and took hold of the last lock of hair.

"No!" I screamed. "Don't take my hair away. Stop! Stop!" But he yanked on it anyway and I felt my soul being ripped from my body. And all my thirteen-year-old friends were laughing at me and pointing and calling me a freak. I couldn't wake up. There was the fright wig mother gave me with its polyester hair sticking out in clownish curls.

"Hey Bozo!" my one-time friends yelled. "Hey Bozo!" "Wake up, Baldy!" "Freak!" "Tranny!"

I woke up. My heart was racing and sweat poured off me. I was in a flat-out panic. I wanted to run. I was crying. Panting. I was trapped in the sheets and couldn't get free. When I finally found my voice, I screamed.

"Daddy!"

THAT BROKE IT. With the word came lucidity. Daddy was dead. Mom was dead. Bradley and Oksamma were dead. For all I knew, the nasty kids at school were dead—at least as far as I was concerned.

I untangled myself from my sheets and went back to the shower. I sank to the floor and spent an hour in there before I went back to bed and I still felt dirty. The image of Bradley's corpse came unwillingly into my mind. 1SB41D1E. Once before I die.

Too late, bastard.

I didn't bother to dry myself. Once I caught myself starting to drift off in the shower, I turned it off and flopped on my already wet bed. I was asleep in an instant.

Damn. I haven't had a nightmare and panic attack in months. Not since meeting Dag.

No respite

SOMETHING WAS THUDDING in my head. I covered it with a pillow and demanded that I go back to sleep. Then the ringing. My stupid cellphone. I struggled out of sleep and finally got the MF thing to my ear.

"Deb," Jordan Grant said in my ear. "Are you home?"

"Yeah, of course," I answered muzzily. "Where else would I be?"

"Come to the door then. We've been knocking forever." The pounding in my head. It was the door. I looked at myself in a mirror and hastily pulled on a wig and a robe. I padded barefoot to the door and looked out the peephole to be sure it was Jordan.

I opened the door. Not only Jordan, but Lars. *WTF? Am I busted?*

"Deb," Lars said as he came into the room. "We thought we should come in person instead of calling you." Panic was setting in. I could feel my breath coming in gasps. *Please don't say what you're going to say. Please, don't.* "Dag passed away about two hours ago."

My whole world collapsed. *Please let this be another goddamn nightmare. Please.*

He was sitting by himself at home. Mrs. Prior found him when she heard Maizie howling. She rushed upstairs and Maizie met her at the door. Dag was sitting in his chair with his eyes wide open staring at his painting with some music by Brahms playing on his stereo. He was wearing the suit I brought him Tuesday and the lavender shirt and tie I bought for him.

All by himself, except for Maizie. *Poor Maizie.*

I don't know what to do with myself. Lars and Jordan wouldn't leave after they told me. Jordan went into the kitchen and fixed coffee while Lars sat on the sofa with me and held my hand while I cried. There can't be any more tears. *Dear God, please let me stop crying sometime soon.*

---

wake

Teri brought some food over. Lars didn't leave until I'd called her. I'm going to float away on all the coffee and tea I've had to drink. I don't know why, but after I called Teri, I called Angel, too. She showed up about noon with Cinnamon. So here we sit—four blondes talking about the men in our lives and who we've lost. We all sat around crying and then laughing.

Cinnamon said she'd tried to seduce Dag at the Condo and finally suggested we have a threesome. She felt a little foolish when I revealed that I was his partner and we were private investigators.

"You mean I could have had him all to myself?" she said indignantly.

"Over my dead body, girl," I snapped back.

"God, please," Angel interjected. "We've had enough of those."

We agreed. Cinnamon opened a bottle of wine she brought and poured us all a glass. It's been so long since I've drunk any alcohol, I wasn't going to have any. But she put glasses in each of our hands and raised hers. "Here's to Jeremy Brett and his girlfriend, Debbie," she said. We raised our glasses and drank. It didn't taste good but it tasted necessary.

"And don't you ever call me Debbie again," I said. "It was all I could do to keep from throwing you off the balcony at the Palomino the first time."

"That's dedication for you," Teri said. "So into her disguise that she spared the life of someone who called her by the one name she can't stand."

"There are others," I said. "But I killed the last man who called me one of those." That set us off talking about what happened at the Condo Sunday morning. The only person I'd told anything to was Jordan and that was just the bare facts. Dag was there, so he knew. It felt good to share what had happened. I mentioned getting hit and having my wig knocked off but I glanced at Teri and omitted the part about it leaving me bald. There were things my friends didn't need to know.

Everyone was amazed when I told them about Dag locking Oksamma on the patio and attacking Bradley. Angel said Davy thought Dag was a berserker when he clubbed him. He's not used to being laid out cold in a fight. I couldn't help but say it served him right after he decked Dag the first night he met Angel. Angel agreed.

"He didn't get any that night, I'll tell you," she said. "I was furious." She paused and picked up her story again. "I can't believe Dag tracked me in Minneapolis and I never saw him. He must have been a master of disguise. I'm sure I would have recognized him if I saw him."

That got us off on talking about disguises and I told them I could disguise myself so none of them could recognize me. They really couldn't believe that.

Angel and Cinnamon left about four but Teri stayed and was determined to spend the night, so what could I do?

I FINALLY GOT to bed. Teri and I stayed up watching *Gone with the Wind* on AMC. She's out on the sofa now with a blanket and pillow. I told her to go home and she said she couldn't. She'd get a DUI. I don't know how many bottles of wine we drank or where they came from. I'm going to regret that in the morning.

Jordan called to see how I was doing and later, so did Lars. I haven't laughed and cried so much all in one day—sometimes all at one time—ever.

I really can't have any tears left but they seem to keep leaking out of my eyes. I should drink some more water. I'll be dehydrated.

I don't know what I'm going to do. I was totally irresponsible today, just wallowing in my own grief. Tomorrow, I have to go to the office and clear things out. I suppose there are people who should be contacted. I don't even know where to start. I know so little about him. I never intended to get involved with him—not that I was in that way—but I ended up loving him so much. He was an anchor and a guide and I'm going to miss him.

I do miss him.

Tomorrow, I'll have to sort through papers. Jordan said he'd pick me up to go to the funeral home if I wanted. God, please don't let it be Johnson & Sons. There must be something I can do. I'll solve his last riddle for him. I've got three sets of numbers.

F8ed2d1e, 36Dboobs, and 1sB41d1e. Is it a code? What am I supposed to do with these, Dag? I don't know what to do.

Oh, I feel sick.

In the words of Scarlett, "I'll think of it tomorrow, at Tara. I can stand it then. Tomorrow, I'll think of some way to get him back. After all, tomorrow is another day."

Hung over

I NEVER SHOULD have done that. What on earth inspired me to drink God-knows-how-much wine with Teri, Angel and Cinnamon yesterday? I woke up in the bathroom with Teri pounding on the door. She had to get ready to go to work. Oh! How could she do it?

There was already coffee made in the kitchen and I started rummaging through the shelves for painkillers. I don't keep many but I have aspirin in my purse. Don't ask me why. I always carry aspirin and Band-Aids. I got back to the kitchen and Teri shoved a glass of milk at me. I popped the aspirin and took a big glug of milk, then headed back to the bathroom.

"WTF was that?" I asked when I re-emerged five minutes later.

"Milk and cayenne," she responded nonchalantly. "It's the best cure for a hangover known to man."

"It was a waste of two perfectly good aspirins," I said. The truth was, I did seem a little clearer.

"Look, you can go back to bed or sleep on the bathroom floor all day if you want, but some of us have to go to work." Work. I guess officially I don't have a job anymore. My employer—my best friend—is dead. Stupid leaky eyes. I suppose I need to go to the office and clean up, anyway. I'll do it later today.

"And don't forget your bet," Teri said as she was grabbing her coat and heading out the door.

"What bet?" I asked. *Oh, no. This is one of the many reasons I don't drink.*

"You bet Angel, Cinnamon, and me that within the next month you could have an interaction with each of us in which we had no idea who you were. You were bragging about how good you are at disguise. So, by Christmas you have to show us evidence that you had direct contact with each of us and we didn't know who you were. Should be pretty easy for a master of disguise," she smiled. "Toodles!"

Me and my big mouth.

{4}
Cleanup on Pier 61

I LEFT FOR THE OFFICE after taking most of the morning to sober up. Last time I drank was after my parents died five years ago. Any pattern there? Never again.

———————+++ + ———

The letter

I WAS DRESSED and halfway out the door before I realized I was wearing jeans and a T-shirt. *Damn!* I might not have a job any longer but it was still Dag's office. I went back and changed into a black business suit—slacks, white blouse, jacket, sensible shoes. I put on the same blonde wig I've come to identify with since I started wearing it a couple of years ago. I knotted a scarf around my neck and went out to catch a bus downtown.

The office was cold and empty. Silent. I didn't bother to open Dag's door. I couldn't bear to look into his office without him there. First, I'd check email. Come to think of it, there was paper mail lying on the floor inside the door. I needed to check that. I wondered if there was a protocol I should follow about opening company mail. No one had actually told me I was fired, so I figured the best thing to do was carry on business as usual.

That meant throwing away the junk mail and opening the one remaining piece. It was a check from FinCEN for the work Dag did last month on a laptop Jordan brought him. As usual, it was made out to D.H. Investigations for Computer Forensics. I could take it to the bank and deposit it like normal. I slid it into a desk drawer to deal with on the way home tonight. Or on Monday if need be. I'd not gotten far into email, which was mostly just subscriptions and a couple of messages regarding my research thesis, when a man showed up in the doorway.

"Excuse me," he said. "I'm looking for Miss Deborah Riley?"

"How may I help you," I said, straightening behind my desk.

"I'm John Allen of Allen Jackson Attorneys at Law," he said, presenting a card. It looked legitimate. In fact, now that I thought about it, that was the name of the law office I took Dag to last week.

"I suppose you want me to vacate the premises," I said. "I just came in to clean out my desk. I'm not taking any company property."

"No, no," he answered. "You completely misunderstand me. Lars Andersen is the executor of Dag Hamar's estate. I'm quite certain he wants you to stay on and continue working. I'm sure he'll be in touch with you soon. I'm actually on my way to meet with him now."

"I don't understand." I'm pretty dumb when I don't want to listen.

"Dag came to my office last week and made revisions to his will. I'm not at liberty to discuss them with you because that is the responsibility of his executor. But I am confident that after he reads Dag's will, Lars will want you to remain here and keep this business functioning until it is properly distributed to Dag's heirs. But there *are* things that lie outside Dag's will, which I agreed to execute on his behalf. The thing I have for you is completely within the legal rights of the deceased, so you needn't worry about this being legal." I was intrigued. Did Dag leave me some instructions that he wanted me to keep working on? Well, yes. He wanted me to collect the other code from the tattoo and put them together for him. But I assumed that came to an end with his death. The attorney was plunging ahead and I struggled to keep up with him. That's one thing about attorneys—you don't really have to hold up your end of the conversation.

"Dag asked me to personally deliver a letter to you," he went on. I nearly choked. "I do not know the contents of this letter but I have some non-official advice for you. I strongly suggest that whatever its contents, you keep them to yourself until after Dag's estate has been settled. It is personal correspondence between Dag and you and does not have any bearing on how the estate is settled or how it is accounted. No doubt it contains information about his feelings for you or, since you were his employee, someone he wants you to personally notify. It might even contain instructions for his funeral. In any case, read it in private and should you have questions about any portion of its content, you may contact me and discuss the matter under attorney/client privilege. Is that clear?"

"Yes," I said. Frankly, I didn't understand a word of what he said but it sounded like he was going to give me a letter and I should keep my mouth shut about it.

"Here you are," he said and handed me the letter. Then he left.

I sat for a long time with it in my hands, just staring at it, not sure that I wanted to know its contents. Dag was sending me a letter from the grave. "If you are reading this, I am dead…" That sort of thing. Opening it would hurt.

I decided to put it away until later—perhaps when I was at home and in private. I shoved it into my purse and went back to cleaning up the office.

Clue me in

I FINALLY CONVINCED myself to find out if Dag had left any kind of list or directory of people who should be contacted in case of his death. I cleaned out his desk and made sure there were no paper notes around. Then I just sat on the sofa looking out at the Sound. I heard a noise in the outer office and a moment later, Jordan's voice.

"Deb? Are you here?"

"In here," I called back. Jordan's frame filled the doorway and he came into the room.

"How are you doing?" he asked gently. *JFC! I'm not a damned China doll. I'm not going to break.* It sounded so patronizing.

"Fine."

"Must be tough to come in here and not have Dag sitting at his desk," he said. I realized he wasn't just comforting me but he missed Dag's presence as much as I did. I waved him to a chair. "Brenda has a bail hearing on Monday. It's likely she'll be released," he said. That was like a blow in the gut. She tricked Dag into killing Simon. Dag went to the grave with that knowledge and it was devastating. It was so unfair that she might be released after all the harm she's done.

"Bitch."

"We have Simon's computer and the backup disks Dag made. They were in the Condo when we raided Sunday. I just had a funny feeling though, based on things Dag told me I should always look for. Maybe the computer was tampered with—not by you or Dag, mind you—by someone before it was brought to you. If that were the case, I'm betting there are backup disks for the computer someplace. Dag taught me a long time ago to always look for the backups. People delete things from their computers if they think someone is going to look at them. But they don't change the backups," he said and paused. I just nodded. Something about what John Allen said earlier made me think I shouldn't say anything about what Dag and I were investigating, even to Jordan. Self-preservation told me I shouldn't admit to having the backup disks, whether he knew or not.

"I've got a warrant to search Brenda's house to look for backups. I'm thinking I'll hold onto it for a couple of days. It would be much more impressive to let her get home on Monday and serve the warrant then. I'd like her to be home when we come after the disks so she has a little extra fear to deal with." He paused again and looked out the window at the ferry pulling out of the terminal. "I'll look like a royal fool, though, if there's nothing there to find." He let the words trail off, then added, as if to himself, "Yep. A real fool."

Okay. With the remnants of a hangover headache and admittedly unclear thinking, I was detecting that Jordan was throwing me a bone. If I could get the backups returned to Brenda's house before he went in with a search warrant, he wouldn't be coming after me.

"I'm sure you'll find them," I said. "You guys are really thorough with your searches. I bet you won't have any difficulty finding them. She's so conceited, she probably has them in her desk drawer." There. I basically told him exactly where to look.

"Do you think so?" he asked. "It's good to get a second opinion on these things. I mean, you were a big help in examining the container that had counterfeit CDs in it. If it hadn't been for you and Dag telling us to follow it, we might have missed the whole bust."

I smiled at him. It was a sad excuse for a smile but I like Jordan and if I can help him nail Brenda's hide to the barn wall, I'll do it.

"If you need anything, Riley, you've got my number. Maybe after things settle down a little, I could take you out to dinner as a thank you for all the help you've been on this case. There's a good possibility we might work together again in the future, don't you think?"

"If I can get a job someplace, sure," I said. "By the way, do you know of anyone else that should be contacted? I was just looking through Dag's address book but there aren't that many people. He went to visit cousins in Sweden in September. I'm just trying to put together a list."

"I don't know but I'll bet that someone over at the Swedish American Center would know. Maybe they'd even post a notice."

Of course. I'd dropped Dag there. It's where he spent every Saturday afternoon. I'd even joined him for Thanksgiving. Everyone there knew him and was his friend. I knew right then what I'd have to do tomorrow.

If I've got the courage to do it.

{5}
Telling the friends

I KNEW WHAT I HAD TO DO. They were the friends I'd seen dote on Dag as if he were some kind of Ballard hero. But it took all my courage to get in the car and drive over there.

––––––––|–|–|–|–||||||||||–|–|–|–|–––––––

Knäckebröd and risgrynsgröt

ON THANKSGIVING, DAG took me to the Swedish American Center for the most spectacular day I'd ever had. I saw him talk to people he'd known all his life, even though he didn't speak Swedish. They knew his parents and some had known Dag since he was a little boy. I also knew that every Saturday afternoon he went to the club to play cards and to eat dinner with those who gathered. It was the only family he had as far as I knew, and no one there had been told he passed away.

On the way, I stopped at an international deli and picked up knäckebröd, a kind of Swedish cracker. From what I gathered, it was what Dag contributed to the weekly dinners. When I passed the center, looking for a parking space, I could see people inside playing games and sitting in front of a TV. I was sure the Seahawks were playing. Or maybe they were out of season and it was someone else. I should pay more attention.

I parked but couldn't get out of the car. I was terrified of going into the center by myself. These people had all been so warm and welcoming to me at Thanksgiving, but I was with Dag. I wasn't one of them. I knew that and even though Mrs. Seafeld arranged to put the almond in my dish of risgrynsgröt, it was all to please Dag.

When I finally managed to pry myself out of the car (It was getting cold!), I didn't walk toward the club. I walked around the neighborhood, just looking at the little houses on the hills of Ballard. The streets were hardly wide enough to drive down but cars were parked on both sides. At every intersection there was an island in the middle that you had to drive around. Even in the cold air, children were outside playing, sometimes in steep yards and sometimes right out in the middle of the street. I walked about thirty minutes before I realized I wasn't anywhere near where I thought I was. I retraced my steps, seeing everything again for the first time.

A ball bounced out of a yard in front of me and I instinctively bent to scoop it up and toss it back into the yard to the waiting towhead little kid who was laughing and running toward me. He screeched in laughter as the ball got to him, scooped it up, and threw it to an equally blond friend up the slope.

But something caught my eye in the shoveled sidewalk. I knelt back down for a closer look. My heart caught in my throat when I saw scratched in the cement, "Dag '03". No. It wasn't my Dag. But some little boy had scratched his name into wet cement. I could easily imagine Dag having done the same kind of thing when he was a child. These streets were his home. He probably grew up near this very place. Oh, don't get me wrong. I wasn't making a saint out of him and revering the neighborhood he grew up in. But it really got to me that this was his neighborhood and his neighbors would want to know about him.

I quickened my steps back to the Swedish American Center, took my knäckebröd firmly in hand, and walked in.

———————+++++++||||||++++++———————

Black coffee

IT TOOK A few minutes before anyone realized I was there. There was activity everywhere. Guys were playing cards in one corner. Women were playing board games with children in another corner. The TV was blaring. It was getting dark out and inside it was like watching a huge family gathered together on a winter's evening. I could see a few older people, men and women, in the kitchen preparing who-knew-what delicacy for the table tonight. After spending a few minutes invisibly standing near the door, I decided to start with the men at the card table.

"Excuse me," I said as I approached.

"Shh, shh," one said without looking at me. He raised a finger to me while another led a card, each played their last cards and they were scooped off the table by the winner. It could have been pinochle or whist or spades from what I could tell. The man who had hushed me now looked up at me and said, "Yah sure, what'll you have?"

"I was wondering if you are the gentlemen who usually play with Dag Hamar on Saturday afternoon," I said.

"Well, when he shows up now, he plays here. Now look here," he said to his companions and called across the room. "Lena! It's the young woman Dag brought to Thanksgiving." People suddenly stopped what they were doing and turned toward me. A few, including Mrs. Seafeld, who I recognized from the dinner, actually came over to where we were standing. "Where's Dag, Miss?" he continued to me.

I really thought I was going to get through this without crying but my damn leaky eyes took it on themselves to nearly drown my words when I spoke.

"I'm sorry to bring you this news," I said. "Dag passed away Thursday morning. I thought you should all know." I was dripping tears out my eyes and my nose was running. I thought they were all going to just stay silent when Mrs. Seafeld wrapped her arms around me and said something in Swedish. I nodded my head and said, "Thank you," and everybody in the room started laughing and crying all at the same time. I handed Mrs. Seafeld the knäckebröd. "I hope I got the right thing. I didn't want you to be without since you didn't know about Dag," I said.

People milled about as word was passed back to the kitchen to those who hadn't heard and the TV was turned off. I was led to a chair and made to sit while everyone gathered around and asked questions about what had happened. Someone pressed a cup of black coffee into my hands and I sipped greedily at it, feeling the warmth and stimulation sink into my nervous system. I answered the questions the best I could. I told them how Dag had rescued me Sunday morning and had fought to stay alive for three days to get a new heart but it proved too long a wait.

What a difference! My girlfriends got me senselessly drunk on red wine when they came to comfort me. Inside half an hour I was so wired on black Swedish coffee that I couldn't stop talking. I told them everything that had happened since I met Dag six months ago and, in turn, they passed around stories of his childhood, military service, business, and card playing. It seems they all remembered a time when he'd hit a baseball into the stands at a Little League game and hit the loathed math teacher in the head, when he'd had a double run in spades with a thousand aces, when he moved away from Ballard to Seattle (as if it had been another country), and who he dated in high school.

"That would be me," a woman said nearby, raising her hand. "I'm Rhonda Somvar," she introduced herself to me. "Dag and I dated in high school."

"You…." I said and hesitated. "You painted the picture."

"What picture is that, dear?" she asked.

"A seascape at sunset with a man on the beach."

"You've seen that?" she laughed. "A childish effort, I'm afraid."

"Dag loved that painting," I said. "He… He died looking at it."

"Oh, my!" she said. "I knew it was bad but I didn't think it would kill him!" Everyone laughed, including Rhonda, but I could see there were tears in her eyes, too.

———————————

I THINK I'VE been to a wake. Someplace along the line we ate dinner, including the knäckebröd I brought, spread with thick slices of cheese. The dinner was different than Thanksgiving. For one thing, there was a turkey. They said no one had thought of it on Thanksgiving but they were determined to have one sometime. Still, it had an abundance of butter, gravy, and potatoes, and many little casseroles that I couldn't identify. We told stories, even while I was helping wash dishes.

I can't imagine there being another memorial service for him that could be more fitting, though Reverend Olson offered to speak to the funeral home about the arrangements. I didn't know who was in charge but I told him that Lars Andersen was the executor of the estate and John Allen was his attorney. He said he would take care of everything from there.

I did the right thing. I went to his family and told them. His family happens to be a whole club of people who share a neighborhood and heritage I scarcely knew existed before I met Dag. I was invited to return each week—even though Mrs. Seafeld took me aside and showed me an entire kitchen cabinet full of unopened knäckebröd packages and we had a wonderful laugh about Dag bringing another one every week—but I know it won't be the same to go back again. I love them but they were Dag's family. I can't hang onto that for the rest of my life.

That reminds me. I've been hanging onto this letter for a whole day now. I'm afraid of what I'll read in it. I'm afraid no matter what it says, I won't be able to take it. Well… I was afraid of the Swedish American Club, too. I guess there's nothing to do but face it.

Soon.

{6}
Playing Santa

I'M SITTING IN A COFFEE SHOP in Madison Park watching the locals come in for a Sunday morning coffee and newspaper. I'm lucky there's a connection. I blend in perfectly with the surroundings here—just another Sunday morning blogger. I can see three other laptops from where I'm sitting.

I'll bet none of them got here directly from breaking and entering, though. I've got to break this habit.

———————+++++++++

Breaking and entering

I GOT UP at five after way too little sleep. The coffee buzz from yesterday afternoon kept me up past two. But I didn't wake up puking my guts out, unlike Friday.

I got into my cat burglar outfit, which is remarkably like my running clothes—black leggings, black hoodie, running shoes. I chose a short brunette bob wig for my hair of the day, or at least the morning. Then I drove to Madison Park and parked my car at a public access point. I focused on looking and acting like any other early morning runner, only there weren't many running in the dark at six on a foggy morning. Fog is good. It means it's marginally warmer this morning than it's been the past few days. It also means I become invisible much more quickly when I'm headed away from someplace or someone. After I'd warmed up, I took only the tools that fit in my oversized waist pack beside the backup CDs.

It was about a mile to the access point I'd identified a couple of weeks ago. A path led from the water's edge on Lake Washington up to the Barnett house. Since I was coming up from the beach this time instead of the front drive, it was much easier to slip up to the house without a chance of being observed.

The last time I was here, I didn't care if Brenda found out or not. I just disabled the alarm system and left the door to the garage wide open. This time, though, I didn't want to raise suspicions when she got out of jail. I took the second story entrance. In my brief visit two weeks ago, I noticed a balcony off the master bedroom above the kitchen. It overlooks the pool and the lake. I had also discovered there were no motion detectors and only the lower level doors and windows had alarms.

I hoisted myself over the railing on the deck, having first checked carefully to be sure no one was coming up the jogging trail. It took only thirty seconds to pick the lock on the French doors and get into the bedroom. I closed them behind me and stood looking around the room.

I rushed my last visit, focusing all my energy on Simon's office where I found the backup disks. I was here today, only to return said disks so certain law enforcement officers could find them. But with Bradley dead and Brenda in jail, I had leisure time to see if I could leave anything else suspicious where Jordan could find it. I had no idea what it would be.

The bedroom was disgusting. A laundry hamper was full and there were dirty clothes on the floor around it. An elaborate bath was marred by makeup scattered around on the sink without particular regard for order. I could see a huge bottle of lilac-scented toilet water. The odor in the room made my eyes water and I'm not nearly as sensitive to scents as Dag is. Was.

A bedside table had an open drawer with various adult toys shoved into it. The bed was unmade and velvet ropes hung from the corners to the floor. The bolsters for the bed were lying on the floor in a corner and the spread lay in a pile at the foot of the bed. The walk-in closet was crammed so full of clothes and shoes you couldn't walk into it. No matter what image Brenda attempted to portray in public, the bedroom painted a picture of a lazy, messy person. Brenda was a slob. I headed for the stairs down, keeping a careful eye out in case I had missed a motion detector.

Someone—housekeeper?—had cleaned the rest of the house. Apparently, the bedroom was Brenda's private domain and she didn't allow even the housekeepers in it. I'd rethink that rule if I was her.

I continued to the office and carefully replaced the disks in the exact place I'd found them. I was trusting that Jordan would arrive with his search warrant soon after Brenda got home from the hearing Monday and she wouldn't have time to look for the backups again. Just in case, I'd downloaded everything onto the servers on Friday.

I searched the desk for any other evidence of Brenda's wrong-doing but to no avail. I looked everyplace I could think of for a safe but also found nothing. The house outside the bedroom was so immaculate and spotless, you'd think no one lived there. There were no dirty dishes and no clean ones in the dishwasher. No food in the refrigerator either—not a quart of milk or stick of butter. It looked like the house had been cleaned for sale but the owner still occupied one room. I was glad I'd slipped surgical gloves on before I entered. Dag used them to protect sensitive equipment when he disassembled a computer. I used them so I wouldn't leave fingerprints. In a house this clean, one solo set of prints that matched me would be incriminating.

I checked every drawer in the dining room sideboard, the linen closet, the utility room. If there was a safe in this house, I knew not where. I finally gave up and headed back to my exit through the bedroom. I opened the drawer on the other side of the bed from the toy drawer but it contained little other than reading material and pencils. I glanced back at the drawer full of toys and it hit me. This drawer was less than half the depth of the toy drawer, yet from the front it looked the same. I carefully removed the contents of the drawer and pulled it out of its guide.

It definitely had a false bottom and when I shook it gently, I could hear things sliding around in it. I turned the drawer over and saw a little twist screw on the bottom like you would see on the battery cover of a laptop. I used a penny from my pocket to twist it open and the lid came off. I'd hit the jackpot.

In the drawer were three complete sets of identity papers, passports, credit cards, birth certificates, marriage certificates, and a sizeable amount of cash in 100-dollar bills and 500-Euro notes. Everything in the house made sense now. It was cleaned to evacuate. The last room to be done was the only room Brenda had been using since... well, probably since Simon was killed. Brenda was prepared to run. My guess was that if Jordan hadn't stepped out of the closet to arrest her Tuesday, she'd have been gone by Wednesday morning.

I copied all the information from each document in my notebook. The identity kits were complete for both Simon and Brenda. Sets this good must have cost a fortune. One set showed them as residents of Belize, one of Bangkok, and one of Monte Carlo. The names were all different. Two of the sets showed them married with the same last name and marriage certificate from the country in which they lived. The third was for two single people.

I replaced the contents of the drawer and put it back on its track in the bedside table. Looking around to make sure I hadn't missed anything, I retreated out the balcony doors and made my escape. I ran back to my car and moved it to the coffee shop where I'm supposed to meet Teri by nine o'clock. I see her coming in now for our Sunday adventure.

As if I need more!

Message from the grave

TERI AND I had a good time. We went to a little French Bistro for Sunday brunch and then went out to catch the first matinee of *Déjà Vu*. Yeah, I'm a sucker for action films if there is a good plot and a good lead actor. It was fun. And Denzel Washington! Yow!

Here's a concept. Everyone went ballistic when they put Daniel Craig in as a blonde Bond. How about casting Denzel Washington in the role of Bond. Now I'd really be a Bond girl for that!

I got home about five and had a message from Lars. He wanted to set up an appointment to meet at my office as soon as possible. I called and offered to come up to see him but he said he really wanted to come down to the pier for this. Absolutely wouldn't say what it was about.

It could be that I haven't done a damn thing on my thesis for two weeks, including have any meetings with him. But why at the pier?

It got me thinking and I went into my bedroom to find the envelope Dag's lawyer delivered to me. Yes. I'm a huge chicken. I finally went to sleep last night with it still in my hand unopened. I decided I had to do it now. I curled up on the bed with it and slit it open.

I'm not going to tell you everything word for word. John Allen said it wasn't a good idea. But here's a couple of things. There's a long string of numbers followed by his name and mine. There's a page of what he thinks is on Simon's thumb drive. I couldn't believe he deduced all his guesses based on the limited amount of actual knowledge we had but it is definitely a wow! And then there was this page.

I realize now there are things I never got around to teaching you. Maybe some of them I did. I'll review.

First, you can do it. It might look impossible at first but I have faith in you. It's not a big business but it is a good one. If you decide to stop, be sure to dismantle everything. Don't leave a trace left.

Second, being clever, smart, and pretty won't always be enough. Sometimes you'll just have to be lucky. I'm hoping you will always be lucky. You'll improve your luck if you decrease the risks you take. It's easy to go prowling around when people don't know you are there and just take what you need. But you will be luckier if you limit the amount of breaking and entering you do.

Third, the law doesn't always define what's right but we don't either. Whenever you decide to do the 'right thing' and it's not the 'legal thing,' well... let's just say I've made my mistakes. The whole BKL thing was probably a mistake. I think we were manipulated through the whole thing. Doing what seemed like the right thing wasn't even a smart thing.

Fourth, find good people to make up for your weaknesses. I'm not accusing you of having weaknesses but I know that when I found you, I made up for a lot of my own. I'm hoping you can find a partner who will back you up the way you've been there for me. Doing it all alone isn't nearly as much fun as doing it with a good partner. It's a lesson I learned way too late in life.

Fifth, I know it's been the hardest thing I've tried to teach you but anything you can find out about someone else, a better hacker can find out about you. Take your security seriously. Don't leave files, passwords, access codes, or anything else on your computer. You have a memory; use it. No one can subpoena what exists only in your head.

There are a couple of last things I'd like to ask you to do for me. There's a letter addressed to my cousin Teresia in Sweden in the vault. Write her a note and tell her I'm gone. Enclose the letter. She'll let the rest of my cousins know. There are a few other letters there—things I've kept for people that need to be returned. Please send them on. I've left instructions that I be cremated. They'll give the ashes to you if you ask for them. There's a beach on Whidbey Island just south of Deception Pass. You'll recognize the place when you see it. Scatter my ashes to the wind and water. I'm finally going to find out what's out there.

I wish I'd been thirty years younger when I met you, Riley. Knowing you has been one of the best things to happen in my life.

There you have it—the important part of it. Apparently, Dag figured out a way for me to keep working here. That's probably what Lars wants to talk about. He's the executor of Dag's estate.

I have to go to bed now. My stupid eyes are leaking again.

{7}
Bailed out and over my head

I'VE BEEN SITTING at the courthouse for an hour and they just started the hearing on Brenda's bail and release. Because it's federal, she didn't get the fast release she threatened last Tuesday. I feel so bad for her having to sit in an actual jail for a week! Boohoo.

Catch and release

I SAID 'Hi' to Jordan when I came in, but mostly these court cases are a lot of sitting in the back of a big room in which almost all the action takes place at the front in very quiet voices that no one in the audience can hear. There's no jury. It isn't a trial or even a hearing. This is where the two—or if I'm counting correctly, six—lawyers argue with each other over whether it is safe to trust her on her own recognizance and how much bail is adequate to assure she won't jump bail.

I could give them a tip—she's going to run. Jordan already suspects that. All they can do is argue about making it as costly as possible for her to leave and then watch to see if they can catch her. A condition imposed was that her passport be surrendered. After another hour of haggling up in front, the judge pounded the gavel and announced bail had been set and paid, and Brenda was released on her own recognizance. There was a stern lecture to the prosecution regarding having an airtight case on the software counterfeiting charge in two weeks or he would dismiss it.

Jordan finally separated himself from the prosecution team and came back to sit beside me. The judge called a recess for lunch with the next case to be heard at two o'clock. Before long we were the only ones still sitting in the back of the courtroom.

"Well, the game's afoot, as Sherlock would say," Jordan said. "She's being followed and I'm heading out to be near Madison Park when she gets there. We don't want her in the house for long before we move in with the search warrant."

"She's going to run, Jordan," I answered.

"She's going to try," he smiled. "This is a federal case and her passport has been collected. She would be stopped at any border."

"Any wagers on that?"

"No. But, despite what our judge said, we've got an airtight case against Barnett, Keane, and Lamb and she is the major shareholder. Bradley Keane's wife holds a twenty-five percent share now that he's gone. I'm sorry her retirement fund is looking a little weak at the moment. She seems like a nice woman. With Simon out of the picture, Brenda holds the remaining seventy-five percent." Jordan paused. "I shouldn't do this, but do you want to ride along for the search? You'd have to wait in the car until we're done but I wouldn't mind the company."

Was he making a pass? What an exciting date to ask me out on if he was. Either way, I wasn't in the mood for it at the moment. I just wasn't able to socialize with business interests right now.

"Sorry, I've got an appointment back at the office with Lars," I said. "Why don't you call me next time you're doing a drug bust? I'd really like to ride along for that."

"You know I don't do drug busts," Jordan answered. Apparently, my sarcasm was too subtle. Jordan's a nice guy but you know what? Sometimes he's a little dense.

"You know what you could do sometime?" I asked. "Stop by with the file on this case, especially Brenda's profile and arrest record. I'd just like to scan through it once for clues on where the real money was going and where it was coming from."

"That's probably just a little out of bounds," Jordan said. "But I never turn down help from D.H. Investigations." I bit back a response that D.H. Investigations was out of business now that D.H. was dead. Jordan didn't deserve that and it's really just my bitterness showing through. I want Dag's last month on earth to have meant something. I was afraid the whole thing was going to blow over and the person he fingered as the culprit was getting away.

I left the courtroom and headed back to the office.

———— ++++++|||||||++++++ ————

Last will and testament

EVERYTHING STARTED POPPING about the same time this afternoon. Jordan called and told me they recovered the backup disks from Brenda's home office. She was furious. It was a pleasure to watch her rant about planted evidence but she couldn't deny those were backup disks for Simon's computer. They were all neatly labeled and were in the desk.

Unfortunately, the warrant had limited scope. They could search for backup disks to the computer and once they found them, they really couldn't search the house for anything else. He thought Brenda's housekeeping was amazing. I kept my mouth shut.

The funeral home called to ask if it was okay for Reverent Olson to lead a memorial service on Wednesday. Why were they asking me? He must have given my name to them. Could I stand another memorial service? I hoped Dag wouldn't mind the Lutheran minister praying for him.

And then Lars showed up. He hemmed and hawed a bit and insisted we go into Dag's office to chat. He looked around the room and made a few notes. As executor of the estate, he had to place a value on Dag's possessions. He'd already been to Dag's apartment and knew about the Mustang. He pulled Dag's little laptop out of his briefcase and set on the desk. He returned to the sofa and faced me.

"His affairs were very tidy," he said. "He left the list of his accounts and policies attached to his will. He wasn't wildly wealthy, but he lived simply and frugally. There won't be much tax on the inheritance."

I started to mention the vault but Lars cut me off before I could say anything more.

"There's no mention of a vault in the will. I believe he wanted his ashes scattered." I started again but he cut me off again. "There is no mention of a vault," he said with finality. "Now, we should really read the will." I was totally confused.

"I thought wills were read by the attorney," I ventured.

"Yes. In fact, it was. I'm the executor of the estate, so I'm the only one who was there for the reading. From that point it is up to me to contact the heirs, report the value of the estate, and distribute it according to Dag's wishes."

"Why do you want to read the will to me?" I asked. Maybe I'm dumber than the blonde wig I wear would indicate. I really had no idea.

"Because two weeks ago, Dag visited his attorney and changed his will. The change made you his sole heir, Deb."

I sat staring at Lars like an idiot. I'd heard those words before. Five years ago, an attorney told me I was the sole heir to my parents' meager estate. There hadn't been all that much. The house was mortgaged. Dad had a retirement plan but Mom had drunk most of the liquid assets. The car was wrecked. Because it was a good market, I made enough on the sale of the house to finish paying for college and get into grad school. That was it.

I remember thinking when I got that check, this was all that was left of my parents. Their entire lives had amounted to a check for $50,000 and a collection of rare whiskey bottles.

And me.

I couldn't bear to see Dag's life reduced to a few numbers on an accountant's ledger. Why was he doing this to me?

"Deb," Lars was saying softly. "Listen to me. I didn't send you to Dag to get involved with him or to become his heir. I sent you to him because he was the best graduate I had and you are the best student. This inheritance isn't about money. It's about carrying on. It's about becoming all that you are capable of being. It's not about making you into a memorial to Dag Hamar, either. It's Dag's way of saying how very proud he was of you and how much you meant to him."

"But I can't even run the business," I wailed. "I don't have a license."

"He thought of that. He called me while he was changing the will and asked me to hold the agency license until your three years is up and you can apply for it yourself. Since I'm fully licensed, I can act as your supervisor, just as I did for the first two years. In May, you'll be able to take the exam and the State will license you independently. The business license is not the same as the Agency license. As a business, you can continue to do computer forensics in this office as long as you want with no PI license at all. As soon as I file the papers, the business license and all its assets belong to you. And

I'm going to file the papers as quickly and as simply as I can. As far as I'm concerned, you are now the owner and operator of D.H. Investigations."

Lars left the office a little after six. He left me staring out at the Sound in the darkness and the fog that was gathering over the waterfront.

Suddenly, I understand why Dag spent so many hours staring out this window.

{8}
Getting down to business

ALL TOLD, it was a better day. 'Better than what?' you ask. Well, better than sitting in my room crying. It appears that I still have a job—or a whole business—and I'd better take care of it.

—————++++++++++++++—————

Encrypted cryptos

I SAT IN the room I will always think of as Dag's office. If what Lars told me is true, it was now my office. Lars would take care of the books and hold the agency license until I'd completed my three-year probation and tested but he promised the business was mine and he would hand over the accounts as soon as he verified them and reported the inheritance to the State. So, it wouldn't be fair to Dag if I didn't get some work done.

I opened the vault and located Simon's thumb drive. I knew right where it was. I'd filed it when I transferred all Simon's backup disks to the network. I might have returned the original backups to Simon's desk for Jordan to find but I kept the data. Something told me there was data on those disks I'd need, even if I succeeded in cracking the encryption on the thumb drive. I shoved the drive in a slot on the workhorse computer, closed the vault, and sat down to work from the laptop. Like Dag would do.

I now had three 8-digit numbers. It should be easy to put them in the right order to crack the encryption. F8ed2d1e, 36Dboobs, and 1sB41d1e.

It took a couple of tries before I realized I was dealing with hexadecimal numbers and not case sensitive passwords. f-8-e-d-2-d-1-e-3-6-d-b-o-o-b-s-1-s-b-4-I-d-i-e. The '5' was 's' and the 'O' was 'zero' and the 'i' was a '1'. It was a kids' game to make up words out of letters and numbers. Being hexadecimal, he only had the numbers 0-9 and the letters a-f to work with. Any eight characters would yield a 128-bit encryption key. I had to believe each tattoo had the characters in the right order. Typically, you double, double, and double again with each added character. But even though the encryption strength was something in the neighborhood of four million bits, I only had to deal with eight possibilities.

Just like Simon, according to Dag, to create a super-strong encryption key and then reduce it to something simple.

So, what did I have to work with? I decided to try all combinations of the sets. I figured the key would not be a scramble of the 24 characters but could be any combination of the sets of letters. Order counts. It could be set 1, set 2, set 3 or set 1, set 3, set 2. The same was true moving set 2 to the first position and combining with 1,3 or with 3,1. Finally, it could be set 3 with 1,2 or 2,1. But what if it didn't use all three sets? What if I had to pick the right one or the right two. A total of eighteen possibilities.

I tried plugging them in when the drive launched and asked for the key. Fifteen straight failures. We'd already tried the first one alone. I plugged in the other two and still nothing. I looked at the original notes. Dag had written the first two on a notepad in the hospital in his neat, precise lettering. The last one I photographed off Bradley's dead body with my cell phone. I examined all three to see if there were any other letters that I could substitute for the numbers or sounds in the words. I came up blank. I didn't know what Simon's and Angel's tattoos looked like, but if they were like Bradley's, there must have been some elaborate artwork. Could that be a clue? I didn't have enough data.

It was way past lunchtime and I was famished.

Driving Miss Maizie

ABOUT MID-AFTERNOON THERE was a gentle knock at the office door. I called, "Come in," and Maizie came bounding across the office and leaped into my lap at the desk. She began vigorously washing my face with her tongue. I was laughing as I looked up to see Mrs. Prior.

"She insisted that she wanted to come to the office," Mrs. Prior said. "She's been going on about it since Sunday. I told her, 'Give Miss Riley a chance to get her bearings, now. Don't rush things.' But Maizie has a mind of her own. I finally had to give in and bring her down here."

"Oh, Maizie," I said. "You are wonderful. How could I not have thought of you without Dag? It must be terrible." Maizie lay down on my lap and put one huge paw over her nose and whined.

"She misses Dag," Mrs. Prior interpreted. "She was worried about you. She thought maybe you were gone, too."

"No, Maizie," I answered. "I'm here. And it looks like I'm going to be here for a while. You can come and visit anytime you want."

"Mmmhmm," Mrs. Prior stuttered. "You see, about that…" Oh, no. She was going to tell me that Maizie couldn't come to visit. I'd miss her so much. How could she do such a thing? "Maizie was Dag's dog," she continued. "According to Mr. Andersen, Dag left everything he owned to you. That means Maizie is your dog now."

"My??? Oh, my." I was floored. I know my stupid eyes were watering again. Maizie lifted her muzzle and licked my cheek. How can I ever hope to be all Dag expected of me?

"Maizie jumps up and down in pink ribbons when she thinks of you," Mrs. Prior said. "I think she is very happy you are hers."

"But I can't keep a dog in my apartment," I said forlornly. "It's a no-pets building."

"Well, dear, Maizie and I understand you need some time to adjust. No one expects you to move straight into Dag's apartment tomorrow. I'm happy to sit with Maizie when you can't have her with you but she hopes you will come to stay with her soon." Mrs. Prior talked so much like I expected Maizie to that I sometimes forgot Mrs. Prior was in the room. "Maizie goes upstairs at night to sleep, even though Dag isn't there," she said. "She is so sad. This is the happiest I've seen her since Wednesday night when Dag got home."

"Do you want me as your pet, Maizie?" I asked the dog. After the past six months of hearing Mrs. Prior talk about her and to her, I no longer doubted they communicated. "I'm not as good as Dag, but I'll take care of you."

"I see pictures of…"

Maizie jumped down from my lap and danced in circles on her hind legs.

"Well, I guess I don't need to interpret that. Why don't you two have a nice chat this afternoon. You can drop her back at my house when you leave for the day and I'll keep her at night. You need to come and look after your apartment sometime."

"My apartment?" I suddenly saw new images in my mind. Dag had not left me just the business, he left me his entire life. Mrs. Prior was telling me that I could move into his apartment. The big question was 'Could I?'

"I'll bring Maizie up around seven if that's all right," I said. "We have food here for her dinner." As if I had just given her permission to be here, Maizie ran twice around the room as fast as her little legs could carry her and then settled on her bed behind the sofa.

"She likes to walk, you know," Mrs. Prior said. She waved a cheery goodbye and left.

———————————————

I WALKED MAIZIE home about six-thirty. We went by way of the post office so I could mail the letter to Dag's cousin in Sweden. I resisted the temptation to read what he'd written. Sometimes I'm too nosey. This time, I'd just let it pass. It was between him and his cousin. I wondered if she was nice. I hoped I would hear from her sometime. Half a dozen other letters were there and stamped, so I took those to the post office as well. I couldn't help but look at the names. A couple of the letters weren't addressed, so I'd left them in the vault. I assumed these were people he'd done work for and kept material that needed to be returned. I wondered what he'd done for that cute up-and-coming actress in LA. Or the woman in Thailand. Well, those mysteries were none of my business.

Maizie and I walked up the hill toward Dag's apartment and as we passed a coffee shop, Maizie pulled on the leash, sat in front of the door, and refused to go any farther.

"Come on, girl," I coaxed. "That's a coffee shop. They don't allow dogs in there." She refused to move and I saw the barista come out from behind the counter and approach the door. I braced for a lecture on pets in eating establishments. The door opened.

"Maizie!" the woman exclaimed. "How are you, little girl?" Don't you want to come in for a biscuit?" She looked at me curiously. "Where's Dag?" she asked. *Oh no.* Another person who needed to be told. It was always so hard to say the words.

"I'm sorry," I said. "Dag passed away early Thursday morning. I've been trying to contact people he knew but I didn't know he was known here." The barista's eyes glistened at the news.

"Oh. Are you his…?"

"Business partner," I supplied.

"Won't you come in," she said. "I owe Maizie a biscuit."

"If it's okay," I answered.

"Oh yes. Until recently, Dag stopped here every morning on his way to work," she said, leading us to a table. "You say he died Thursday morning? He was in Wednesday evening. Said he'd been out of town and that was why we hadn't seen him lately. I'm Jackie, by the way. Would you like an espresso?"

"Thanks," I said, "but I shouldn't do caffeine this late in the day."

"It's okay. I'll make us decaf." She brought a dog biscuit and Maizie sat on her hind legs patiently while Jackie gave it to her. Rather than crunch it up immediately, Maizie carried the biscuit to the other side of my chair, turned around three times and settled with it between her paws. Then she took a bite.

Jackie brought me a straight espresso in a demitasse and sat down opposite me. I learned that Dag and Maizie stopped here at Tovoni's every morning on the way to work and had done so up until a couple of weeks ago. Then she hadn't seen him until Wednesday night. He looked very tired but she loved to watch him drink his coffee. He seemed transported.

The sneak. He knew he wasn't supposed to have coffee. Not for the past six months. But he'd been coming in here every morning anyway. I had to laugh as she told the story. I told her the time and place for the memorial service tomorrow and then walked Maizie the rest of the way home.

"What else are you going to tell me about Dag?" I asked her. She seemed very proud of herself.

When we got to the apartment, I knocked on Mrs. Prior's door to tell her we were there. She motioned me up the stairs and told me to take my time. Maizie led me up to Dag's apartment.

It was so much like it was after Thanksgiving when I'd spent the night on Dag's sofa and he'd touched my head and comforted me. God! How I wish I could have comforted him. I didn't know until that week how sick he was.

Everything in the apartment was clean and neat. I walked from room to room. I looked at pictures. I touched his clothes. I ran a hand over the top of his bed.

I'd made a lot of decorating suggestions to Dag, knowing he'd never take me up on them. Other kinds of suggestions, too. But here I was, feeling more intimate with him than in any of our playful conversations.

I sat for a few minutes in his chair and looked at the painting on the wall. It wasn't terrible, like Rhonda thought of it. It was a little primitive but it did have a way of capturing your thoughts. I'd sat there for almost an hour before I decided it was time to go home and go to bed.

I'm going to have to take this in little doses. If I try to swallow it all at once, I'm sure I'll die.

{9}
Farewell, friend

EVERYONE SHOWED UP. Lars and Jordan, of course. Everyone I'd ever met at the Swedish American Center and dozens more. Teri came to be with me and I wasn't surprised to find Angel and Cinnamon there, too. The four of us—blondes in black dresses—must have looked unusual to many who were there, based on the number of stares we got. There were so many blondes among the Swedish contingent, I don't think we were at all out of place. Maybe it was just the way our dresses fit.

In memoriam

I SAW THE obituary and funeral announcement in the paper last night but I had no idea how many people Dag touched. There were people there he must not have seen in years—certainly not in the past six months. Reverend Olson gave a kind eulogy that didn't come across as too religious. It was really about Dag.

People at the Center had put together a display board with pictures from various events over the years that showed Dag playing cards with the older men and sitting on the floor amidst a huge pile of Legos with the children. I thought he would have made a great dad. There were pictures of him teaching computer classes filled with older people at the Center and a beautiful picture of Dag at the top of Mount Rainier taken by one of his climbing buddies twenty years ago. It was so incredible to see him as a young man, so full of vitality and so… sexy. There was really no other way to put it. Dag as I knew him was kindly, sophisticated, and distinguished. The young Dag was nothing short of a hunk.

I made my own contribution to the display. I had the picture of the two of us, taken in a photo booth on Pier 57, blown up and framed. I also brought the seascape painting from Dag's wall and set it in front of the memorial urn that held his ashes.

It was all about remembering the wonderful things Dag was to so many people.

And then it was over.

Lars pulled me to the doorway of the chapel and there, flanked by my blonde posse, people stopped to offer me condolences as they left. He explained people needed a focus for their condolences. They treated me like I was his widow. Sometimes it was embarrassing to imagine what they must have thought but everyone was polite. Rhonda stopped and held my hand for a long moment while tears streamed down her cheeks. Eventually, she pointed at the picture she'd painted and just mouthed, "Thank you," and then left.

Another blonde in black stood before me. I was a little in awe. Cali Marx had come to Dag's funeral.

"You must be Deb Riley," she said softly. I nodded. "I know I'm probably no older than you, but you remind me of my mother. That's not fair but Dag was going to be my father before Mom died. I hope you don't mind that I hope they're together now." Dag was going to marry Cali Marx's mother? *Damn!*

"Of course, Miss Marx. Uh… If you'll forgive me, Dag had an envelope in his vault with your name on it but it doesn't have an address. If you're staying in town, I could have it couriered to you."

"I'm still not ready. Are you continuing his… business?"

"Yes. I was his partner and inherited the bulk of his estate."

"I paid Dag a retainer to keep that envelope until I need it. Can I trust you to do the same?"

"I will always honor all Dag's commitments," I said. She handed me a personal card with an address and phone number.

"Dag told me about you when he came to the premiere of *Donovan* in August." The movie hadn't been a big success but Cali Marx was sensational.

So, that's where Dag went when he said he had business in LA. "He told me about his brilliant new assistant. It was obvious that he was in love, even then. Please update my file and continue to hold the envelope for me."

"Yes, ma'am."

"Come on. I'm not that old. I'd love to stay and chat, but I practically had to commandeer an airplane in order to get here. I don't dare keep them waiting to fly me back. Please let me know when you plan to scatter his ashes. If it's possible, I'd like to be there." She lifted her veil. Despite the tear tracks on her cheeks and the smeared mascara, she was incredibly beautiful. "I loved him, too." She kissed me on the cheek and then left. I saw a limo waiting outside the doors of the funeral home. She stepped in and was gone.

IT WAS OBVIOUS my buddies weren't intending to leave me alone for a while but Jordan managed to cut me out of the crowd when I went to retrieve the urn.

"I've brought you something," he said. "I don't think I should be giving this to you but I'm going to file a statement that this is official business." He handed me a manila folder filled with the dossier on Brenda. "She's gone," he said flatly. "We don't know where or when but we haven't seen her come out of the house in two days. I got a warrant and we went in this morning on the grounds of being concerned for her well-being. She was gone. The entire house was immaculate save the bedroom. It had been ransacked. We determined she had packed one suitcase and left. The other matching pieces were on the bed."

"Can I say I told you so?" I asked. I suppose it wasn't kind but I had told him Monday morning she would run. He'd lost her that very day.

"I'd rather you said you'll help find her. I can bring you the laptop and backup disks if you need them but I'm betting you either know where she is or could find her."

"And then what?" I asked. "Are you telling me there is enough evidence to get an extradition from an unfriendly country?"

"No. I'm saying you will find the evidence." Jordan looked around. "Dag and I didn't share everything either of us knew," he continued quietly. "But we shared enough that I'm sure he was onto something more than Bradley's little scheme to counterfeit software. I'm guessing you are pursuing his leads. We always had a tacit agreement—don't interfere with each other and we'll share the results. And don't go in without backup," he finished.

"I suspect that the two billion Simon disposed of before he got himself killed is just the tip of the iceberg," I answered. "If so, there's a Titanic about to find it."

"I'll bring the laptop and disks by this afternoon," Jordan said.

"Don't bother," I answered "If your crew hasn't found anything, it's unlikely I will." He looked at me a little strangely but said 'okay.' I told him I'd let him know if I found her and how bad it really was.

———— ++++++++++++++++ ————

I TURNED TO join my friends. They wanted to take me out for a drink but I said absolutely not. Instead, we four went down to the pier and they joined me in the office. Mrs. Prior brought Maizie to the memorial service and handed me the leash before I left. The five of us sat on the sofa and chairs and I set the urn in front of the window.

"Ginger snaps for everyone," I announced, getting the jar from the desk. Dag liked the crisp spicy cookies. We each reached in and I tossed a cookie to Maizie. She took it to her bed and lay down. We all took a bite. There were various expressions ranging from disbelief to disgust. "I guess they're an acquired taste," I said, laughing.

Let's just say Maizie had a lot of treats that afternoon.

———— ++++++++++++++++ ————

Carrying on

AFTER ASSURING MY friends I was all right, I got them out of the office and settled down to do some work.

The databases of United States Customs and Immigration are not exactly public but they aren't impenetrable either. I knew, if I wanted to, I could get into them and find out if there was any record of Brenda's travel under her aliases. But the truth is, we don't check on people leaving the country. We only check those entering. The fastest way for Brenda to get out of the country was to go to Canada. There's always traffic moving across the border and a middle-aged woman crossing from the US to Canada isn't going to raise any flags if she has some cockamamie story about going to Vancouver to shop for her grandchildren.

But Brenda didn't take her car. That meant she took some form of public transportation (or had a confederate hook up with her) and the most likely place to go would be the airport. Once there, she could either rent a car or board a plane. If the choice was the latter, it didn't make any difference where she went. Out of the country was out of the country. That's what I was betting on. I pulled up the OAG online guide and looked at the flights normally leaving from Seattle with non-stops out of the country. There are a lot. It was all guesswork. I figured she would head south rather than to Canada. It was always possible she could catch a flight to Amsterdam or Tokyo but I couldn't picture Brenda risking a really long flight. She would want to be on the ground someplace by the next morning.

Airline passenger lists are harder to hack into than US Immigration. Mexican Immigration, however, is a breeze.

I set up routines to scan every port of entry with direct flights from Seattle, starting with the last time Jordan actually saw Brenda. There are twenty-one different international ports of entry with direct flights from Seattle. Four are in Mexico and six are in Canada. The rest are scattered throughout the world. I entered the passport numbers from the three identities I'd seen in Brenda's drawer. Someplace, one or more of those people were going to show up entering a foreign port. The number would be scanned and entered in the immigration database.

It wasn't child's play. Before I finished, I had to take Maizie out for a walk and feed her dinner. She was getting impatient when I set the programs to run and started pulling apart Brenda's file.

Huge chunks of written evidence had yellow stickies on them marked 'circumstantial,' 'unconfirmed,' and 'hearsay.' I had to admit the case against her looked shaky. No wonder Jordan wasn't getting any support from authorities on his search for her; they considered it a waste of time.

The ferries were almost shielded by the nighttime fog over the harbor by the time I found something useful. If you commit a burglary, speed, rape someone, or even murder someone, they are going to do a pretty thorough job of marking down your identifying characteristics and getting your fingerprints. Age, weight, height, eye and hair color, race. But if you are accused of a federal money crime, your file is going to include birthmarks, shoe size, ring size, moles, and tattoos.

'Tattoo at the base of spine in red and black depicts a pillow with the characters El8d2bMe.'

Damn! Brenda had a tattoo with eight characters. An 'l' had to be a '1'. The 'M'? It had to be a 3 laid on its side. Elated 2 be me. I had a few more combinations to try out for my encryption key. Let's see, with four sets in all possible combinations of one, two, three, and four sets… I only had sixteen possible combinations when there were three sets. There were sixty-four possible combinations with four sets. It was going to take a little longer but I just doubled the possibilities for the encryption key.

It's going to be a long night.

{10}
Breakout

T HAT MFSOB! If he weren't dead, I'd find him and kill him myself. "Simon Says," my Aunt Fannie!

———————————————

Decryption

I FOUND THE combination of 32 characters that, when put together in the right order, made an encryption key. If you are interested, it is 15b41d13f8ed-2d1e36db00b5e18d2b3e. Here's a bit of advice. If you get hold of this MF thumb drive, don't enter the encryption key!

Fortunately, the damage was limited.

I was being lazy and too excited that I'd found a possible breakthrough to be careful. Dag had plugged the thumb drive into Simon's computer even though it might have an ill effect on the computer. It was isolated behind a million layers of firewall and protection, so we tried. I decided to take security one level higher when I started working on this and did a bit-by-bit copy onto a new thumb drive. It's just standard. We always work with backups and I think there's even another in the vault. I hadn't looked for it, so it was just as easy to burn a new one. I don't have Simon's computer now, so I put the new thumb drive in Dag's laptop.

You have to understand that Dag's laptop (Lars gave it to me after the hospital gave it up) doesn't have anything on it but the routines he used to connect to the virtual private network. It doesn't connect to anything automatically, so it's a pretty safe clean computer.

I sat in the office carefully inserting the drive, getting the dialog to enter the encryption key, and trying the next one on my list. These are hexadecimal keys, so there aren't any capital letters. Each character is a number from zero to fifteen. It's pretty common in encryption keys. But you have to be exact, so I worked slowly. I didn't have to try them all. I hit pay dirt about three-quarters of the way through the list. The dialog box closed and for a minute I wasn't sure what to think. I launched a directory window and took a look at the files on the drive. One executable.

Everybody with an elementary education knows not to launch an unknown executable on your computer. I adjusted the directory settings to show hidden files. Voila! I could see dozens of files but they were all still encrypted!

That's when all hell broke loose.

The screen dissolved into a lot of little dots and resolved itself into a moving tickertape message. The message was juvenile at best.

"Simon says, 'Find me if you can.' All the clues are here. Everything you wanted to know. I never expected you to get this far but I'm not making it any easier to uncover the secrets contained on this drive. It's too bad you're colorblind, Dag!"

You are dead, bastard. And so is Dag. How dare you taunt me from the grave?

The screen dissolved again and a new message appeared. "Press Esc to continue."

Everything else on the computer was locked. Nothing responded. I pressed Esc. The message that returned said simply, "You lose! Simon didn't say 'Press Esc.'" What a childish game he was playing. Or so I thought. The screen rewrote with rolling text. It didn't take long to realize it was deleting all the files on the disk, starting with the thumb drive and proceeding to the laptop. It was totally wiped in seconds. I unplugged, disconnected, ultimately had to pull the battery on the laptop in order to stop the action, but the damage was done. I had to reformat the laptop and start it back from scratch. Fortunately, the bios wasn't damaged. The thumb drive, once destroyed was worthless. It had no file directory on it and showed as empty. I ran a few recovery tools and it's possible I could have recovered it but there's no real need to. It was a copy.

———————|–|–|–|–|–||||||||–|–|–|–|–|———————

It's two in the morning. I'm going home. I'll take Maizie with me and go to sleep. At this hour, no one will know she's there. I've got other things to attend to tomorrow.

———————|–|–|–|–|–||||||||–|–|–|–|–|———————

Travel funds

Some things have to be done face-to-face. I had no doubt that if I simply asked Angel how she helped people move money, I would get a straight perfectly accurate answer that was worthless. Might as well Google it. The only thing I could think of was to take a wad of cash into her office and get cash cards. Except she couldn't know it was me.

I disguised myself as a male. It took about two hours to get the mustache and hair on correctly. It had to be perfect because I had to look like my ID. This hair was glued on a transparent latex base. It's a baldpate fringe. When people look for a disguise, they focus on the forehead. A flip of your hair in the wrong direction will show the wig foundation. They don't see a line at the forehead on me, so they don't look at the fringe of hair I glue on to look like a man with a really receding hairline. It's better if I have Stevie help me with this. She's a master. She's the most intimately acquainted with my head and my various wigs as my hair dresser and confidant. She's a former theatrical makeup artist as well and has helped me into any number of disguises. Today, though, I was all on my own.

I suited up in a houndstooth tweed jacket with a turtleneck shirt and a sweater. If you aren't stacked—as if I'd ever have to worry about that—the easiest way to hide your boobs is with bulky clothes. It's December and it's cold out, so that doesn't look strange. I've got an undervest that is padded to fill the valleys and give me just a little more breadth in the shoulders. Don't forget the fingernails. I keep mine short anyway but make sure all signs of polish have been stripped away and the nails are dull, not shiny. Unless I get strip-searched, no one can tell they aren't looking at a man. The final thing to add is just a hint of shadow around the cheeks. Even when a man is clean shaved, he normally has hair growing on his cheeks that affects the color of his face. I needed the appearance of manliness that diverts attention away from the narrowness of my nose. Finally, I added a pair of steel rimmed glasses. They're slightly tinted and make it harder to see my eyes.

When I was done, I checked my appearance against the photo I had on my James Whitcomb passport. It was a match and even looking in the closeup mirror, I couldn't tell I had makeup on. It was showtime.

I DEBATED A while on the amount of money I should take with me. One of the first things I discovered in the vault was a stash of cash Dag kept for just this kind of operation. There was a lot more than I would need. I carefully counted out $12,000 in hundred-dollar bills. I didn't want to be too loaded but from what I'd observed at Angel's office, I needed to have a significant amount of cash to transfer.

I drove over to Dag's apartment and let Maizie in through the secret door without going into the apartment. I didn't need Mrs. Prior asking questions right now. Fortunately, she was out and I slipped in and out in no time.

I parked in the Macy's lot and walked six blocks to Angel's travel agency. It's a little mindboggling to walk naturally through a non-great part of town with twelve grand in your briefcase. I elected not to use a bag with a strap because that too often signals a woman. I just kept my head up and strode along with purpose.

I felt a frisson of anxiety as I turned onto her block and disciplined myself not to look around for threats. The best defense is alert confidence. At any rate, I made it to Angel's door a little before noon.

I was in the lioness's den. Approaching it from this side of the counter, it looked considerably different than it had when I observed her operation from the other side. She had taken all requests for cash cards into a private office. I approached the counter. I thought Angel looked stressed but the moment she looked up at me, her expression changed to absolute charm and hospitality. When Angel switches on her sex appeal, it even affects me. She's that kind of gal.

"Good morning. How may I help you?" she smiled at me.

"Morning," I said quietly. Bravado is not the right mode for me when I'm playing a man. I pitched my voice a little lower and softer than my normal. Angel instinctively leaned in closer. "I need to buy a cash card for vacation. I heard you sold them."

"You heard right," she replied easily. "How much would you like to put on your card?"

"Would $12,000 be all right?" I asked.

"Sure," Angel said, leaning over and flashing an abundance of cleavage my way. No wonder men drool over her. She came back up with a form and pushed it to me over the counter. She seemed to be looking past me part of the time and it gave me the feeling that I should turn around and look at what was outside her window. Instead, I shifted my focus to look at the surface of my tinted glasses. I could see the reflection behind me but no one was there that I could tell. I did see the shadow of two or three people pass by the window but no one stopped.

"You need to fill out this form completely and I'll need your ID," she smiled. I hemmed a little bit as I scanned the form. This was a government form and I wasn't crazy about writing down the information they asked for.

"Is there a way to do this without all the paperwork?" I asked quietly. "I have poor handwriting."

"Are you now or have you ever been associated in any way with any branch of law enforcement at local, State, or National level?" Angel surprised me with the question.

"I got a parking ticket once," I confessed. "Does that qualify?"

"A simple yes or no is the only answer I want."

"No." Angel went from intense to welcoming again. "What's the big deal?"

"You cannot lie to me about that and use anything we say or do as evidence in a legal case," she responded. "Even if it is being recorded on a wire." My mouth worked of its own accord in stuttering denial. "Just hand me your wallet and passport as if we were conducting business normally," she said, "and then step through the door over here to my office. We'll complete your transaction there."

I fished my wallet out of a back pocket and my passport out of my jacket. I pushed them through the grate to her and obediently waited while she went around a partition. That's another part about an effective disguise—accessories. You need foolproof identity, of course. I'd learned in an elementary class with Lars how to get identification. But the big issue in pulling out a wallet or getting searched was what was in it and what it looked like. I'd picked up my wallet at a Goodwill store when I first started putting this identity together. There were three signed credit cards in the worn wallet that I'd made sure were worn enough to look used. They were legit, but none had ever carried a balance after activation. They all had expiry dates several months apart. There were also a few easy to acquire membership cards—grocery store, sports club, frequent flyer—and business cards, both my own and a car dealer where I'd had work done, an accountant, and another professor. Some were tattered and had numbers written on the back. The piece de resistance was an official-looking photo ID with a reader chip, identifying me as a faculty member at a local university. The card wouldn't get you through a door at the university but it looked official. And cash, of course. Forty-seven dollars in various denominations, well worn.

A moment later there was a soft buzz and I pulled the door open to walk through. My identity was apparently sufficient for her.

I don't know what I expected Angel's inner office to look like. She'd taken only two of her several customers into it the day I observed and I couldn't see in. It looked more like a psychiatrist's office than a banker's. A small table with two chairs, a short sofa, and an easy chair facing it. A floor lamp provided illumination, even though there was an overhead fluorescent turned off.

The room was also dead. Closing the door behind me cut out all outside noise. When Angel spoke, her voice barely crossed the room to me. I sat on the sofa where she directed me.

"You're new at this, aren't you?" she said. I nodded. "I like to bring new customers in here to explain the menu and to counsel. Privacy is best for our transactions. I assume you have cash to purchase your cards with?" Again, I nodded. "Well, James, there are restrictions the Federal government has imposed on cash transactions. Any transaction over $5,000 has to be reported on one of those forms you were concerned about. We'll break your purchase down into smaller chunks that I can report without arousing suspicion. There is the small matter of transporting money in excess of $10,000 out of the country. It's not illegal, but it is supposed to be reported. Do you understand the problems we have?" I was determined not to speak unless I had to. For all I knew she was recording everything. I nodded again.

"All right," Angel said. She moved out of the chair and sat on the sofa next to me, laying a hand on my shoulder. "My agency provides a world of special services to important travelers like you," she purred. "Especially to travelers who need to move larger sums of money. I'll bet this is just a sampling of the kind of money you want to take care of, isn't it?" I considered a moment then ever-so-slightly nodded, turning my face away slightly.

"Sometimes you have to travel. What do you teach, Mr. Whitcomb? Or should I say Professor?" she asked.

"Literature. Uh… just Mr." I wasn't comfortable with Angel getting any closer.

"No tenure, huh? The bastards." I couldn't believe the way Angel was playing me. She was seducing me into her web—becoming a sympathetic co-conspirator. She moved closer and I decided I had to get space between us. I moved away a bit and turned to her.

"No offense, Miss," I said softly. "I'm not comfortable with women. I prefer… well, you know." When rejecting a sexy woman, the gay card is the best one to play. Angel got the message immediately. She moved back to her chair.

"Oh, don't worry, James," she said. "We can still be friends and you'll find I still have a lot of services I can offer you." There was a subtle change in Angel's gestures and her coyness. A flick of the wrist. A new tilt to her shoulders and erectness to her posture. Her voice came down a notch as well and had a subtle sound of being softened, as though she was just pretending to be a girl. In an instant she had transformed herself from sex goddess to drag queen. I was learning more about Angel than I ever imagined. But I still needed to know how the money operation worked.

"Thank you," I said. "You are an angel. How can I get my money to Europe without arousing suspicion? There's nothing illegal about it," I hastened to add. "An inheritance, you see."

She cut me off.

"I don't need to know where it came from," she said. "I'm not complicit to any source of income no matter what you do. I'll help get it to a transportable form for you. Now, here's what we're going to do to solve your little problem. When there's a lot of money, everyone wants a piece of it," she continued. "I'm not a bargain basement deal but I am high quality. We'll get your money on separate cash cards and you'll have immediate, untraceable access to it in Europe, or anywhere else you want to travel—Asia, South America, or even Australia. And you get all my services for just twenty percent. If you want me to arrange traveling companionship or special transportation, that's extra. Doesn't twenty percent sound like a good deal to you?" She barely waited for my nod before she went on.

"What I'm going to do is give you two $5,000 cash cards. You're going to pay me $2,000 for them. Oh! Look at that. It comes out to exactly $12,000! That will be convenient. I'll report it as three separate transactions. No paperwork. I'll even report it on different days so there is no indication you were here with a lot of money on one day. All you need to do is key in your PIN on the card reader so I can program your cards. You know all the rules about PINs, right? Don't make it your birthday or an obvious pattern. Be sure you remember it because we aren't going to write it down anyplace. Future transactions—You will back to do business with me again, won't you?—will be much simpler. You'll come to the counter and tap in your PIN. I'll take the money and slide a new card through the printer. When you travel, any card will work in the vast network of ATM machines around the world that bear one of these logos."

I was pretty overwhelmed by the time I walked out of the store, $12,000 lighter in my briefcase with two new money cards—one in my wallet and one slipped into my briefcase on Angel's advice. I didn't understand why but she indicated I should not carry my cards too close, even though they had different branding on them. Who was going to find out? Finally, she pushed a handful of travel brochures about various places in Europe into my hand.

Dangerous liaison

I SOON FOUND the answer to my question. I was walking up Cherry St. from Angel's agency when a red-haired man stepped out from a doorway in front of me, flashed a badge and said, "I'd like to speak with you for a moment, sir."

I was facing Jordan Grant in his official capacity as a FinCEN officer.

"Did I do something wrong, officer?" I asked quietly.

"We don't think so but we are investigating the agency you were just in. Would you mind telling me the nature of your business there?"

"Should I have a lawyer present?" I asked.

"We could go through all that," he said, "but I haven't even asked your name. At the moment, I'd prefer to keep our questions friendly and off the record. I'd just like to know what kind of business is conducted there."

"Well, that's easy enough," I answered. "It's a travel agency. I'm going to Europe this summer on sabbatical. I'm a teacher."

"And the woman in the agency is making your travel arrangements?"

"Yes, sir," I replied respectfully. I held up the brochures I still held in my hand. "Italy is going to be magnificent in July. Hot but magnificent. When you are on a school-year calendar, you have to go when you can go," I added confidentially. Jordan, I knew, required a little more male-to-male bonding than I could get away with if he'd been female. The time with Angel was exhausting. This was a breeze.

"And does she charge a lot for travel arrangements?" he asked.

"Well, yes," I said frankly. "I thought for a while she wanted to go with me but—dare I say?—you're more my type." Jordan took an automatic step backward. "Really," I hastily continued, "if she puts together a whole trip package for me based on what I told her, gets me into the Vatican Library and arranges a private tour of the major sites with a native Italian speaker, I think it will be worth it."

"Sounds like it will be a good deal for both of you," Jordan answered. His attention was already distracted by someone down the street and when I turned, I saw Angel leaving the agency for lunch. I did not want to be seen talking to Jordan.

"Is there anything else?" I asked.

"No," he answered shortly. "You've been very helpful. Thanks." With that, he simply walked away in the direction Angel had gone and I continued back to my car.

Whew!

{11}
Perfection

L AST NIGHT, I did something I never do: I slept in all my makeup. This morning, I woke up to see what I would have to do if I maintained a disguise overnight.

———————|—+—+—+—+—++++||||||++++—+———+———|————

The morning after

IT WAS HARD enough to be with Angel while she flirted with me. It was scary as hell to run into Jordan and deflect his interest. The two encounters left me in such a serious panic attack after I escaped from them, I practically ran back to my car, jumped in the back seat, curled up into a little ball, and rocked back and forth while I panted and sobbed. It wasn't even that important. I could have passed off the disguise with Angel if she'd caught me out. I bet her I could have a direct encounter with her and she wouldn't recognize me. Oops. I lose the bet.

I didn't think Jordan would understand as well.

And what was with that? Why is Jordan watching Angel's business and poking at people who go there?

Well, duh. That's easy. She's helping people launder money. What she does might violate the spirit of the law but as well as I can read it, unless they can prove that she's receiving money from some illicit source, she's technically legal. At worst, a misdemeanor. I don't think he was satisfied with my answers about booking travel but it was more important to him to follow Angel wherever she was headed than to keep questioning me.

————————————————

MY MUSTACHE WAS loose on one side, as was a piece of my hair on the left temple. I must have scratched at it in the night. My five o'clock shadow looked like a smear of mud on my face after my cry. I tidied up as much as I could and headed for Stevie's place. She promised to help me perfect the disguise this morning. And believe me, it needed perfecting.

Stevie looked at my hair and makeup job critically. She made a few adjustments and then had me sit in the chair of her salon for several hours while she completely redid everything, lecturing me the entire time. The first task was to make it easier for me to get into the makeup and hairpiece. The second was making it foolproof against detection at close range. If I was going to pull the same ruse with Cinnamon I had with Angel, I would need to get close without being recognized. Even if she didn't recognize me, if she realized I was in makeup and a costume, it would be just as much a failure.

There was no question I'd need to get more comfortable being around girls when I was dressed as a boy, too.

Here's a bizarre question. Who do you think would be more pissed off at me: a straight girl who finds out I'm also a girl or a gay boy who finds out I'm a girl? Oh, this gets so confusing. Why do I feel so obsessed with perfecting my boy act all of a sudden? I should be sitting in my office trying to break the code of Simon's little game or tracking down Brenda. Instead, I'm getting lectured by Stevie on stippling my five o'clock shadow, fastening my hair on, and walking like a man.

When Stevie was finished, I looked incredible. I couldn't even recognize myself. She instructed me to leave the makeup and hair on again tonight and then bring it back to perfection in the morning. Tomorrow, I'm really going to need a shower. I can only imagine what this stuff is doing to my skin. I promised to complete the day today in disguise, seeing and talking to people as a boy. I still need to run by the office though.

————————————————

Wanted

WTF? SOMETHING HAS gone terribly wrong and I don't know what it is. I had lunch on the way to the office and flirted with a clueless teen waitress. It was easily two o'clock when I finally meandered down to the pier. I had in mind a couple more experiments with the thumb drive to see if there was anything on it other than the destructive virus. I had to remember it was all going to be a game of 'Simon Says.'

Before I reached the office, I could hear voices and see my door was open. I started to hurry toward it but realized I had no Deb Riley ID and no proof that it was my office. I didn't want to barge in on a burglary anyway. I approached quietly and listened from outside the door. The voices were from the inner office. The outer office was empty, so I slipped in to hear better.

"Nothing," I heard a voice say. "The place is clean. I don't find a random electrical signal or any indication there's activity in the area."

"It must have been cleaned out," said a second voice. The voice sent a chill down my spine. "Dag did work in here he couldn't have done on the little laptop he carried around. The only person who could have the server is Deb Riley—or at least access to it. We've got a subpoena for the server and a warrant to search the office. We need a warrant for her apartment. I hate to do it, but we'd better get a warrant for Deb as well. We can do it on grounds of wanted for questioning. She must have Dag's research on Simon and Brenda Barnett and I want it."

Jordan Grant was getting a warrant for my arrest? But that wasn't all.

"No one has seen her since the funeral," Jordan continued. "I want all the ports checked. See if you can locate her car. She might have skipped the country already."

I got out fast. I could hear them closing the doors to the office by the time I reached the end of the pier. I thought about my car parked across the street in the Pike Place Garage. It was best to leave it there. But where was I going?

I don't have much to hide from the police but a thorough search of my apartment will reveal some not-exactly-legal ID and all my disguises, wigs, and photos. My heart leapt to my throat. Including photos of the disguise I was wearing. I had to get there before they did.

I flagged down a taxi on Alaskan Way and gave him the address to my apartment. How much time did I have? He couldn't move on the apartment until he had the warrants but he could have it watched. And how fast could FinCEN turn a warrant around? I had a feeling I didn't have much time.

I did a quick drive-by on the apartment and got the cab driver's card so I could call him back. With the $20 tip I gave him, I didn't think he'd go far away. This was going to be fast. I grabbed two big suitcases from my closet and opened them on the bed. Everything that was Deb Riley's had to stay in the apartment. I would be safest if Jordan thought I was still around. But my false IDs, my wigs, my makeup, and photos had to go with me. I pulled all the cash I had out of my hidey-hole in the ceiling of the closet, thinking wistfully of the pile I'd left in the vault.

It's a long story and if I get a break sometime soon, I'll tell you more about it but suffice it to say, I don't have pictures of me with a happy family. You know my history. A bald kid with a drunk mother and an overprotective father doesn't get many pictures taken. Most of them were pictures taken in photo booths in places I'd visited. About eight years ago, I discovered photo editing on my computer. I created the kind of family memories I wanted to have. I used photos of me and me in disguise to mash together a family portrait album with scenes from places I imagined we'd visited. It hurt too much to lose them—my made-up family history. I stuffed every photo I could in my suitcase, removed all the men's clothes, shoes, hats, and underwear from my apartment, and locked the suitcases. I called the cabby and left by the service entrance to the apartment with a hat pulled down over my eyes. I caught sight of Jordan getting out of his car in front of the building just before I saw Hassan's cab pull up.

Where to?

I chose Dag's apartment. It might not be safe for long but for now it was the best I could do to get the break I needed to regroup. I called Mrs. Prior and told her I had a friend in town who needed a place to stay and had given him the key to Dag's apartment. She said it was mine to do as I wished but Maizie was often up there.

When I hung up, the cab driver was giving me an odd look. I realized I'd just made a call with a very different voice than the man's voice I'd been using.

"It's the phone," I said, returning to the masculine. "It always makes my voice sound high. It will be well worth your while if you forget you ever saw me or heard me talk." He nodded. I wasn't sure how much English he spoke. I went back to my phone. It's a pretty sophisticated sleek smartphone. I'd only had it a few weeks but I was going to have to get rid of it. It was Deb Riley's phone. I deleted all my personal information, connection routine, and email from it, called the company and deactivated it, telling them I'd sold it, and pulled the SIM card. I polished it up nicely and when the cab pulled up in front of Dag's house, I handed it to the driver along with a $50 bill.

"You should be able to activate this with either T-Mo or ATT in a couple of days," I said. "It will be really good for your business. Keep the change and lose this address."

He nodded and I escaped with my bags to the sanctum of Dag's apartment. It wasn't more than five minutes after I got there that Maizie pushed the door open and jumped into my lap.

———————————————

So, WHAT'S GOING on?

I've integrated all my men's clothes among Dag's and found a place to hide my pictures but I'm completely cut off from everything right now. I can't be Deb Riley. I'm James Whitcomb. Why is Jordan wanting to arrest me? What does he think I have and why is it so valuable?

I thought that case was closed.

{12}
On the run

I WAS WHIMPERING when Maizie woke me up. I could still hear myself as her wet sloppy kiss nearly dislodged my mustache. Tears were still running down my cheeks as I sat up in bed and tried to take stock of my situation.

—|—|—|—|—|—|—|—|‖|—|—|—|—|—|—

Maintaining an identity

I'D BEEN DREAMING, obviously. I was still caught between that fully submerged state of subconscious synapse firings and objective awareness of my surroundings. The bed wasn't mine but no one else was in it with me except Maizie.

Maizie. I'd spent the night in Dag's bed. I'd fallen asleep with my face buried in his pillow begging a man who wasn't there for help in a problem he didn't know existed. And people who I trusted were trying to arrest me. I felt my head and, for a moment, didn't recognize myself.

I ran to the bathroom and looked at myself in the mirror. I didn't even recognize myself behind the disguise. My makeup was a little smeared from the tears and sweat, but a little touch-up and it was soon put to rights. I took a sponge bath.

I caught a full-length image of myself in the mirror. Unbelievable that this little bald guy with the mustache and goatee had perky little breasts and a tiny waist. And no other accoutrements. Well, nobody was going to get that close a look at me. I had to figure out what to do and where to go. I was pretty sure it wouldn't be that long before Jordan thought to look in Dag's apartment, if he hadn't already.

I selected my clothes from Dag's closet where I'd integrated them. He'd shown me a couple of secret compartments in the closet when I was here over Thanksgiving weekend. He was so proud of all the little gizmos he'd built into the apartment. I couldn't believe he hadn't remembered anything about that day. I'd felt so intimate with him. He was sharing such secrets with me. I opened one of the hidden drawers to put my photos in and saw his car keys. That gave me an idea.

I dressed and took Maizie out. One thing Dag taught me about field work was never to leave anything behind that I couldn't do without. I loaded my pockets with cash, slung my computer bag over my shoulder, and made sure I had all my ID. I packed one compact suitcase with wigs, makeup, essential items of clothing, and an unactivated pay-as-you-go phone. Everything else that might be evidence regarding who I was or that I was in disguise was hidden.

I stopped in the rental garage where Dag's car was stored and dropped off my suitcase. Then Maizie dragged me down the hill toward the office and I reluctantly followed. Her goal, however, was not the office but the coffee shop on lower Queen Anne near the Seattle Center. I slipped into Tovoni's the minute the door was unlocked. It might not be a great idea but I could really use a good cup of coffee.

The barista came around the corner of the counter and stopped short when she saw Maizie.

"Maizie?" she asked. "Is that you, girl?" Maizie obligingly waved a paw and sat up to beg for a biscuit. The barista gave her one. She took it to a corner of the coffee shop and lay down to focus on the treat. "Excuse me for asking," the barista said, "but who are you and what are you doing with Dag's dog?" I'd prepared for this but wasn't that confident.

"I rented an apartment up the hill and the dog kind of moved in with me," I said. "I figured she should be walked and she practically dragged me in here. Could I get an Americano, please?"

She nodded and went to get the drink. I sat beside Maizie and looked at the newspaper. A few minutes later the barista set a drink beside me. I thanked her and took a sip. It was a straight espresso and perhaps the best I'd ever tasted.

"Mmm. That's good," I said without thinking. "I mean... I think I ordered an Americano but this is fine anyway. Thank you."

"Funny, when you were here the other night you ordered an espresso. I must have gotten the drinks confused," she answered.

"I've never been in here before," I said.

"You're good but I'm psychic," she said. Not another Mrs. Prior, I hoped. "You don't have a man's aura about you and Maizie exudes love for you. You are the woman who told me about Dag's funeral. And I've got to thank you for that. He was a good man and I miss him every morning."

"I don't know what to say," I answered. "I'm James Whitcomb. I've never been in here before." Rule number one: When you start a lie, stick to the story.

"Deb Riley," she said. "That's the name. I don't remember people's faces or often even their names. I remember their drinks. You walk in and order one drink and I've got you for life. Take Dag, for instance. He drank what he liked to call a 50/50. It was just an Americano but with the same amount of hot water as of espresso. He liked the crema on top and just used the hot water to keep it hot while he sipped it. You were a straight espresso the first time you walked in and I will always recognize you as that. Dag used to sit in that very chair for half an hour every morning. I'd look at him with his 50/50. I knew when he walked through the door. But I couldn't tell you a single thing about what his face looked like. Don't know what it is. There's a word for it. Prosopagnosia. I just don't recognize faces. I see people's auras."

"How can I convince you?" I asked.

"Well, if you want to be someone else, don't take Maizie with you. There's a magic pairing between a man and his dog. I only say man because you want me to believe you are a man. The pairing is still there," the barista paused. Jackie. That was her name, I finally recalled. "And there was something about your walk. You seemed hesitant this morning. You didn't think it was a good idea to come in here." The door opened and two policemen walked in. "Thank you, Mr. Whitcomb," she said turning away from me and returning to the counter to get coffee for the officers. I continued reading the paper, glancing over it occasionally to see if they showed signs of recognizing me. There wasn't a glimmer. They took their coffee in paper cups and left the shop.

I looked over at Jackie and she smiled at me. "You are safe here," she said. "Anytime."

"Thank you." I paid for my drink and left a generous tip. I never actually admitted to being Deb Riley but I felt I could trust her. We'll see.

When Maizie and I got back up to the house, there were two dark sedans pulled up out front and lights were on in Dag's apartment. I took Mazie's leash off and gave it to her. I pointed to the house.

"Go home, Maizie," I said. "Go on." She hesitated a moment but seemed to get the message. She carried her leash proudly in her mouth and trotted to the door. I turned and headed downhill again, toward the garage where Dag kept his yellow Mustang.

Hiding out

I'M HAVING BREAKFAST this morning at a diner in Cle Elum. I spent the night at a motel here after driving around forever trying to figure out what to do. I finally decided to come across the pass but had to stop in North Bend and get chains for the car before I could make the trip.

Once I was in the motel for the night, I removed all my makeup and got a really thorough shower. When I woke up this morning, I carefully reapplied everything and refreshed the look.

Somehow, I feel safer on this side of the mountains.

THERE ARE TWO things that have me bothered. I downloaded my email this morning and had a cryptic message from a blind address. In fact, my guess is that the account was opened just to send the message. It doesn't seem to have a connection to anything else as far as I can tell.

Ms. Riley: We are informed that you have certain property once belonging to one Simon Barnett. We are certain this property is of little or no value to you but may be of significant interest to a party or parties with whom he did business. We are offering a substantial reward for this property and evidence that any copies have been destroyed. This could be a very profitable proposition for you. Or a very dangerous one should you decline our generous offer. Await our instructions regarding disposition of the property. We suggest you have it with you when we contact you.—The Committee

O-kay. You could be a little more specific, Mr. Committee. What is this supposed property I've got and why do you want it? It makes me mad.

Oh, yes, the other thing.

I got a hit on my tickler. Sandra Ramon entered Mexico on December fifth. It took five days for the information to get through Mexican immigration into the database I was scanning. If I want to find her, I need to get closer and track her on a real time basis. Let's face it. I'm not in a particularly good place out here in Cle Elum, either. If Jordan decides to check Dag's car and finds it missing, I'm sure there'll be an APB out for it in no time. I need to go back to Seattle and store the car again but I don't have anywhere to go.

—————————————

Refuge

THIS IS JUST crazy enough it might work. There's a perfectly good penthouse condo in Seattle currently standing unoccupied. I'm going to make use of it. I don't know if I can stand it but I know I have to try.

It came together for me this afternoon. I kept Dag's car covered overnight with the custom canvas he always kept on it in storage. Seems like a good thing to protect it with in inclement weather and it might also keep it from being spotted immediately.

I drove on down to Ellensburg after I checked out and spent the afternoon in a truck stop restaurant with my laptop open. I needed to find a better location for my base while I sort things out with Jordan. I don't think he's looking that hard for me or he'd have found me by now. He went to the same detective school Dag and I did. So, what's with that? Was he just trying to spook me?

And who is this Committee?

Here's what I pulled together. I tapped into the property management database for the condominium management company. I've leased the Condo from its current owner and am moving in tonight. I found a Kinko's in Ellensburg so I could print my papers, complete with the signature of the property manager. All I needed then was a key, and I figured out how to get that.

It just took a lot longer to manage the pass on the way back than I expected.

{13}
Flirting with a girl

I WAS HALF FROZEN by the time I reached the factory outlet shops in North Bend. I didn't have enough clothes and certainly nothing warm enough for crawling around in the snow under the car to put chains on and take them off. I went through the mall stores picking up clothes to last a week, including something comfy to lounge around in at night.

A way in
THE WEATHER'S BEEN freaky in Seattle lately and I didn't have a good coat, so picked up a warm topcoat. It would be essential to my entry into the Condo. I finally made it to the underground parking for the building, pulled into a row of other cars that were covered, and carefully pulled the tarp over the Mustang. For now, I was only taking the essentials. I figured I'd be able to get back to the car to get everything else later—if I was successful breaking and entering.

I took the service elevator to the next to top floor and got out to hit the rooftop stairs. Dag told me how he got into the Condo when I was being held prisoner there. I understood the rules better this time. Rule number one: Don't get caught. It seems like every rule is number one.

I was prepared for the blast of cold wind that hit me when I emerged from the stairwell onto the rooftop. I immediately dropped to the ground on all fours. What I don't need is to get blown off the roof to a spectacular end of the story.

I crawled over to the edge where I could see the escape stair that led to the penthouse garden. I had one foot on the ladder when I heard the splash below me. A man and woman were getting out of the hot tub—stark naked. She dried him and gave him a robe before slipping into one herself. The two headed toward the pool house opposite the patio doors. I looked that direction and light was spilling out the window from what looked like a party going on inside.

It was only two weeks ago that Jordan arrested Brenda for running a house of prostitution and the place was still open? I wasn't expecting that! I hung there on the ladder for a minute and decided I needed to get down out of the wind, at least. Maybe there would be a chance to get inside as the party wound down later. It was close to nine o'clock now and surely most of these people had to go to work Monday morning.

The office window—replaced since Bradley fell through it—was completely dark. I hoped no one was silently watching from there. I found a sheltered spot in the gazebo, warmed by a propane heat lamp for the hot tub area, and stared through the patio doors. What I saw was awesome. If I had a camera, I could make a mint off the faces I could see inside. Two public officials who ran hard-fought campaigns in November, the president of a major regional bank, and what looked like the entire board of directors of a technology company I owned stock in. The annual report came out in September and I looked at all their faces with some amount of envy.

OMG! I was seeing the holiday party for the Execs! They must have some special arrangements with the bank and elected officials. No wonder the Condo was open to them. Only a couple of faces were missing from the photos in the annual report. Of course, they could be in a different part of the Condo. I didn't know where the guy from the hot tub had disappeared to. It looked like they were getting ready for a toast, so I figured most people were probably there.

Including the girls.

One special girl

ANGEL'S HEAD TOWERED above the others. A guy's face was practically glued to her chest. A few feet away, I recognized Delta. I was cataloging the attendees in my mind when I heard a noise just to my left. I started and she gave a little scream. I held up both my hands to show them empty and harmless.

"It's okay," I said, making sure I'd modulated my voice to its lowest tones. "Sorry I startled you."

"I didn't realize anyone was out here," she said. "Why aren't you inside with the others?" I recognized her voice a second before I saw her face and confirmed I was looking at Cinnamon.

"I'm not really into all that corporate bantering," I said calmly, even though my heart was racing about a million miles an hour.

"I know what you mean," she answered. "I had to escape a certain octopus in there. I swear he had hands everywhere."

"You don't have to put up with that kind of crap," I said firmly, reinforcing something Cinnamon had told me when we were interviewing last month. It was always up to the girl to indicate she was interested in something more than being friendly company.

"It's hard with a gathering like this," she said. "They all expect something for nothing. It's not like when Mr. S was here." I knew the codes the girls used for certain bigwigs.

"Who's running things now?" I asked. "Mr. B and Mr. S have both passed on."

"I don't know for sure but I think Davy Jones is."

"The security guy?"

"Yeah. You know him?"

"We've run into each other a couple of times," I answered. This was valuable information. If Davy thought he was running things, I could manipulate him pretty well.

"Have you been up here before? You sort of look familiar but I can't place you."

"Oh, I've been up a few times but I've mostly been behind the glass," I said, nodding toward the office windows.

"Gee! I didn't realize you were one of the Committee. I didn't get your name."

"James," I said. "You may use Mr. J."

"Can't I just call you James?" she said, sliding a little closer to me. "I mean, when we're alone." Leave it to Cinnamon. If she smells power, she's all over it. I needed a little more information without giving her too much.

"You can call me anything you like," I said, sliding an arm around her waist. I felt a lot more comfortable getting close to Cinnamon than Angel. Angel towered over me and for a tall girl that's intimidating. Maybe I was a dom at heart. Cinnamon is slim, short, and pretty, but I swear when I put my arm around her, she lost every bone in her body. She just melted against me. I needed to press my advantage with Cinnamon and if she discovered who I was, I'd just plead that I was trying to fulfill my bet and lost.

"I've been out of the country for a while, doing work for Mr. S," I said. "Has the Committee been meeting regularly?"

"I don't think so," Cinnamon said. "The girls certainly haven't been called for them. It's strictly been holiday parties. No open member nights."

"Good. That's the way it should be for a while," I yawned. "Sorry. I just got in tonight from Amsterdam. It's already six in the morning there. I intended to stay here tonight."

"We can go in if you really want to," Cinnamon said, laying a hand on my chest. Believe me, I've tested my chest pads often enough to see if they feel natural, but I'm not in the practice of letting other people touch them.

"I don't want to go through the party," I said, glancing at the patio doors where another toast seemed to be underway.

"We can use the locker entrance—through the pool house."

"That's good but I saw someone go in there a while ago. I don't want to interrupt anything."

"Don't worry. They went straight to the red room. He's headed for a massage at the hands of Cascade that will keep them both occupied for quite a while."

We headed into the house through the pool house. It was a dark passage and Cinnamon kept herself glued to my side.

"Which room do you want?" she asked.

"I think I'll go to the office first," I said. "I want to check some records. I'll wait until the party is over before I retire."

"If you like," Cinnamon said, turning toward me, "I'll stay with you and keep you company."

OMG! I kissed a girl! I didn't mean to, but Cinnamon was right up against my face when she suggested staying with me and next thing I knew, she was kissing me. It wasn't a light little kiss goodnight, either. That girl is a serious kisser.

And it wasn't that bad, either. Not really.

I gently pushed her away and felt her hand trailing down my front. I snatched it before she could not discover what she expected to find.

"Cinnamon, baby," I said in a very husky voice with a little tremolo in it. I've heard guys use that sucking air tone after five minutes of foreplay and was surprised how easily it came under the circumstances. "Like I said, I just got in and I'm jetlagged. Let me take a raincheck, would you? I'd like to get to know you a lot better."

"Anytime, James," she whispered back. "Here's the office door. I hope you have your code."

There was a sixteen-key security pad next to the door. I hesitated for a moment and decided to use the one code I was most certain hadn't been changed. E18d2b3e. The door slid open. I started to step inside but turned back and caught Cinnamon's hand. I kissed her again.

It was all for effect… really!

"Cinnamon," I said when we broke our embrace. "I'd rather no one knew I was here until I tell them. You understand, don't you?" I caressed her cheek with the back of my fingers and she melted into the touch.

"You sure are a good kisser, Mr. J," she said. "Anything you say."

I slipped through the door and closed her out.

I stood inside for a few minutes without moving—just listening. I'd plunged forward into this room once before and been surprised with a blow to the back of the head. This time I was on full alert. But no one waited in the room. Not even a scent of lilacs. When my eyes had fully adjusted to the dim light, I went to the window and lowered the blinds. I was not interested in watching the party. I wanted more direct access and I knew how to get it.

I slid behind the desk and opened the security panel. It took only the flip of a switch to activate the security camera monitors in the office.

They no more than lit up than I killed them again. No one was in the room but someone had added a camera since the last time I was here. I moved back to the door and carefully removed the camera from the wall. It was wireless and installed by an amateur. Davy apparently felt he should know what was going on in the head office. I put the camera in the bottom desk drawer and covered it with a throw pillow. Finally, I closed it in its nice dark drawer where it would draw no attention. If he hadn't seen the initial flicker of the security screens in the office, he wouldn't have any idea it was off until morning.

I activated the screens again and watched the party. I examined all the rooms, including seeing Davy at his post by the elevator. The red room was, indeed, in use and I tried to ignore it. That seemed to be the only private party going on.

It was close to midnight when everyone packed up their bonus checks and went home. Davy handed out all the cellphones he'd collected earlier in the evening per Condo protocol. The last to go was Angel. She looked at him with a look that would wither fruit on a tree and he clicked out the lights and joined her in the elevator. According to the security cameras, I was alone. I watched their silent screens for nearly half an hour before I finally allowed myself to relax and prepare for a few hours' sleep.

I started shaking when I realized I'd called Cinnamon by name without her having introduced herself.

{14}
At the helm

I SPENT THE BETTER PART of the day establishing firm control of the Condo, starting with locking the patio and poolroom doors. Then I changed all the security codes from the entrance to the office door. I got my bag from the car and relaxed. I finally feel safe. Relatively speaking.

Security

WHEN DAVY GOT to the Condo he was surprised, to say the least. He stepped off the elevator and his card didn't open the front door. He was swearing so loudly he didn't hear me over the intercom at first.

"Davy! Calm down and follow my instructions," I said.

"Who's that?" he exclaimed, backing up and looking up at the security camera.

"I'm the one who's writing your paycheck now. You can call me Mr. J," I said. "I'll explain it to you when you come in. Yes, I'm going to let you in. But you need to follow your own security instructions. Empty your pockets into the security tray and step through the metal detector."

He tried to get his knife past me the first time, but the metal detector caught it. He finally deposited everything that could set it off and I closed the security tray drawer and locked it. He walked through the metal detector with no alarm and I tripped the security lock on the front door.

"Come back to the office so we can chat," I instructed. "I need an update on the events scheduled this week and I have some errands for you."

Davy was not happy but he was also used to taking orders. In fact, I think he was relieved someone else was running things instead of him. He came directly to the office door and knocked without trying the doorknob first. I buzzed him in and waved him to a chair without really looking at him. I kept my head down, looking at papers in front of me. He sat.

"The place is a mess, Davy," I started.

"The maids were supposed to be here," he interrupted.

"The maids were here," I said. "I'm not talking about the cleaning. I'm talking about the events. The cops dragged out the main computer bank and I'm working with a laptop. Where are you getting the schedule from?"

"The security banks, sir," he responded immediately. "You can get to it with my security code," he continued.

"Is your security code tattooed anyplace obvious?" I asked. It was a long shot but tattooed hexadecimal codes were in vogue this year. He looked puzzled. "Just log me in," I said.

He rose and came around the desk. I slid my chair back and he switched on the security cameras as I watched. I could replicate that. It was obvious he thought he'd been clever. Password, Angel. Rule number one: never use your name, the name of a family member or pet, or birthdays, anniversaries, and social security numbers as your password.

He returned to his seat and I slid back into place. The security camera screen was replaced by a calendar showing the dates of parties. The place had never shut down after our raid two weeks ago. The Saturday night I came to the Condo with Angel, Cinnamon, and Delta for the girls' party, they had talked about the party season. The things you never know till you ask.

"You did a good job getting things up and running after the little incident," I said. "I have a lot of faith in you." I was doing my best CEO impression. Lounging back in my chair was important. Women in big offices sit up straight. Men slouch. I stuck one foot up on the mahogany desk. "Have you heard from any other members of the Committee?" I asked.

"Just Ms. B. She called as soon as… well…"

"Yes," I said. "As soon as you were out of jail? Don't worry. It's not a black mark on your record in this office."

"As soon as I was out. She told me to get things fixed up and make sure everyone knew they were to be ready for the first party that Friday. Then she got framed and was in jail for a while."

"Have you heard from Ms. B since then?" I asked matter-of-factly.

"Yes, sir. I picked her up and took her to the airport when she was free. She told me to carry on until she contacted me again."

"I'm that contact," I said. "In order to keep everything straight, Ms. B gave me a lease on the Condo so I could manage it in her absence. I don't expect we'll hear from her soon. But hey! Together we'll get through the holiday, right?" I asked. A little camaraderie made Davy relax and even smile a little. "I'm representing the Committee while I'm here and we just want things to go smoothly. We don't want to draw any unwanted attention but should things heat up, I'm here to take the heat. A federal agent is watching everything that goes on in the Condo, so I don't want to raise any suspicions." I paused and looked over the calendar on the screen. "Isn't there a Committee meeting here soon?" I asked.

"No sir."

Davy was short with the answer. He acted like it was a test and he was answering according to the stated rules. I smiled.

"Good man," I said approvingly. "Now, here's what I want you to do."

I went over a number of instructions I'd prepared in advance regarding how the parties were to be handled and my changes to the security system. I gave him a new security code that would open the front door during the hours I felt he should be there. I carefully described what those hours should be. He made two adjustments to the times so he could be there when deliveries were scheduled. I approved and sent him off to do his work. Before he left, we had come to an agreement. My presence would be divulged on a need to know basis and the security code on the office had been changed. No one was to come in or out during parties or in my absence.

When he was gone, I started scouring the secure database of information Davy gave me when he logged me into the security network. Next was to find Brenda.

Making nice with Jordan

I CHECKED MY email via my own VPN and found I had a voicemail from none other than Jordan Grant. It's about damn time he called me. It was a short message and sounded friendly for a man who had just put out a warrant for my arrest.

"Hey, Deb! Long time, no see. I've got some of the information you wanted. Give me a call so we can talk. See you."

Information I wanted? The only thing I wanted from Jordan he'd given me in the form of Brenda's arrest file which I had no doubt he'd retrieved when he searched my office. Careless of me. I should have kept that with me but I hate paper. Jordan was trying to get a bead on me through a phone contact. He might have been calling my cell phone, but that chip was safely tucked away in the back of my computer bag. I could reach him, though, and he would have a devil of a time tracking me back.

I logged onto my VPN and called up an internet phone system. I jacked a headset into my computer and called Jordan.

"This is Riley," I answered his curt greeting. He was suddenly all smiles over the phone and I could imagine him directing an army of guys to trace the call. Tough to trace when you are calling a cellphone from a VOIP.

"Deb, I've been worried about you. Where are you?"

"Safe."

"Is something wrong?"

"It's a tough life when you don't know who your friends are, who might be searching your apartment, and who might have issued a warrant for your arrest, Jordan," I said. No sense beating around the bush. I wanted him to know I knew what he'd done. I could hear his hesitation as he decided whether denial was worthwhile. Instead he came clean.

"Look, Deb," he said. "It's for your own good. I wanted you in protective custody. There are things you don't know that could hurt you."

"Why not call and tell me what I need to know instead of trying to make me run?"

"I wasn't trying to make you run. I thought we'd get you in and explain things and you'd be safe. No one has seen you since the funeral."

"I'm safe for now. But I'm on Brenda's trail. You know she landed in Mexico?" I asked.

"No kidding?" He sounded genuinely surprised. "We guessed she'd be headed for Europe. Is she getting ready to fly?"

"Not sure. I seem to be a few days behind her. Getting cooperation from authorities down here isn't easy if you don't have a lot of cash." I thought I'd drop the phrase 'down here' just to see if Jordan would assume I was literally following Brenda.

"I can see if I can pull some strings. If that would help. It's actually a relief to hear you're in Mexico instead of Seattle. Things are getting sticky up here."

"Tell me what's up, Jordan. Maybe I can relate it to what I've found so far."

"There's some sort of syndicate involved in this. We haven't been able to trace it to any known crime family but the activity moving through BKL accounts is continuing, even though the operation is shut down. It's like they have a life of their own."

"It's called the Committee," I said. "Brenda is the chairman."

"You're kidding! Well, it seems they believe there is an artifact that Simon left exposing them all. Word on the street is Simon gave the artifact to Dag. With Dag dead, you default as the main target. We only found out because they tried to get info from the FBI regarding whether they had it."

"Shit," I said. "It's a stupid thumb drive. If the data is on it, it's not going to be known. I have it with me. I'll make a copy and send it to you but be forewarned: It's encrypted with a billion-bit security code and if you get it wrong, it launches a virus that will wipe your machine—possibly spread to the whole network."

"Geez, Deb. Don't you think that's withholding evidence or something? Why didn't you give it to me right away?"

"Independent investigation. I didn't know you wanted what I had. You could have told me," I said. "Dag gave it to me and said to crack the encryption. I share with my partners but my partners don't usually try to get me arrested."

"Okay, it was a big mistake. I'll get the warrant cancelled. But for Pete's sake, keep me up to speed on what you find out."

"As soon as I'm sure there's no warrant, I'll come back to town."

"Just get me the thumb drive. Oh, and one other thing," he said.

"Yeah?"

"There's a new player in town. We haven't got a make on him yet but he's the first new customer Angel Woodward has had in months. I was going to follow him but he didn't seem important enough when Angel made the move to her bank last week. I've a feeling he's more than an errand boy."

"Can't imagine who that would be," I said flatly. "But thanks for the warning. I'll be on the lookout." I wasn't saying if I was on the lookout for the new guy or the tail.

We rang off on friendly terms and I was partially relieved to think the warrant would be off and I'd be able to be myself again. But I still don't know if I can trust Jordan. I want to. I just don't know.

What would you do, Dag? You could give me a little help here.

{15}
Nailed it!

AMAZING WHAT A GOOD NIGHT'S SLEEP will do for you now and then. With the Condo secured, I removed all my makeup, showered, and slept. I had Davy make sure I was supplied with food and coffee before he left yesterday.

———————|||||||||———————

Red letter day

I TOLD DAVY he wouldn't be needed again until party time on Thursday night. Everything else was fine in the Condo. That meant this morning I had time and energy to spend pulling pieces together. I'm monitoring a lot of accounts Brenda had set up and am tightening my grasp of her schedule. I'm guessing she moved from Acapulco pretty quickly after she arrived but if she flew internally, there probably isn't a record I can find unless I search every flight out of Acapulco since she arrived.

I'm hoping her sense of security in having escaped will make her careless. There's sure to be a charge on one of her credit cards or a ticket purchase or a customs record sometime.

In the meantime, everyone seems to think the thumb drive holds the mysteries of the universe and the careers of some very important people. So, I think I'd better get down to cracking it. It's just a matter of waiting for Simon to say what's next.

I WAITED AND now I'm stuck. I plugged in a backup and got the familiar message asking for the encryption key. I entered the thirty-two digits in the order I'd worked out and waited. I got the same message. "Simon says, 'Find me if you can.' All the clues are here. Everything you wanted to know. I never expected you to get this far but I'm not making it any easier to uncover the secrets on this drive. It's too bad you're colorblind, Dag!" Then, "Press Esc to continue." No deal this time, Simon. I waited.

Sure enough, there was a new message popping up after about ninety seconds. "Simon says enter the password." *Oh shit. Now I'm stuck.* If I hit the wrong thing, I risked losing the whole thing again. I looked at the keyboard for a while and pressed the one key I thought might be safe. The computer went into immediate hibernate mode. Now if I can wake it up without triggering anything, I've got time to figure out what the next encryption code will be.

I sat back to think about it for a while. What did Simon's message say? Too bad you're colorblind. Simon knew Dag was colorblind and it affected the puzzle. But how? I was going to have to risk going back to the office. I locked things up and headed for the waterfront. I hoped Jordan was serious about dropping the warrant and no one was watching for me.

IN AND OUT. I can't believe I was so dense. I've got two parts of the mystery and I know where the third is. Then it's on to solving the fourth part. It was all in the file on Brenda. Jordan left it on the desk after he searched the office. I suppose he wanted it to look like no one had been there. They did a good job.

When I read about Brenda's tattoo, it said the tattoo was red and black. Sure enough, the detail said the 1 and d and pillow were red. Everything else was black. I checked my photo of Bradley's tattoo and found two letters on it also in red—the b and 1. If there are two letters in each tattoo in red, they would make up a second 8-character code. What I had so far were the first and last pair if the order of the original tattoos holds true. B-1-_-_-_-_-1-d.

Dag didn't mark any letters on either Simon's or Angel's tattoo as being red. But Dag was colorblind and had never actually seen them. I slipped the SIM out of my James Whitcomb cell phone and inserted my Deb Riley

SIM. The first thing that showed up was a lot of voice mail. I decided to check it before I called Angel. Several calls from Jordan. I have to give him credit. He did try the cell before he tried the office. I still didn't completely trust him but no one had burst into the office to arrest me yet. A call from Cinnamon that was too funny.

"Deb, you've got to call me. I've met a guy and he is absolutely delicious. I don't know what to do. He hasn't called me. I don't dare call him. This is absolutely squeeee! Call me!"

Oh, geez! The call was from early Tuesday morning, right after my last encounter with Cinnamon at the Condo. She is going to be soooo disappointed.

Teri called. "Hey girl, where are you? We were supposed to go up to the pass to ski Sunday. Call me."

The last call was from Angel.

"Deb, this is Angel. Give me a call, would you? Weird things are happening. I've had a dozen people ask about you this week. Some of them are pretty spooky. They know I gave Dag a computer thingy from Simon. If you've got it, get rid of it. I don't think you're safe as long as you have it. Call me."

That call I needed to return right away. I went back to the Condo to make the call. I'm not ready to blow my cover completely.

"Hello?"

"Angel, it's Deb."

"Girl, where are you?"

"Everyone wants to know where I am," I said. "I'm hiding out. What's up?"

"I've had a string of transactions this week with a common thread. An escalating threat of 'action' if I don't come up with details about where that little computer disk thing is that I gave Dag. I'm sorry, Deb, but I told them I gave it to him. Somehow, I thought it would be safe since Dag was dead. But they zeroed in on you. They keep calling to see if I've heard from you and asking me where you are."

"Geez, Angel. Are you okay?"

"Yeah. No. I'm getting out."

"What do you mean?"

"I'm on my way to the airport. Simon left me a nice property in Croatia I'm going to make use of. I'm sorry, Deb. I should be here for you but I'm scared. I'm leaving while I can."

"Don't worry, Angel," I said. "I'd do the same thing. If I show up on your doorstep there, please invite me in."

"Not to worry."

"Angel, one other thing," I said before she could hang up. "It's important."

"Go ahead."

"You've got a tattoo. Dag told me about it but there's a detail he missed. Which two characters in your tattoo are red?"

"The 6 and the first o," she answered. "They're one above the other and Simon had some rather vulgar jokes about putting them in that order. He could make a dirty joke about just about anything," she answered. "Look, I'm at the airport and I've got to run now. Good luck, Deb."

"Thanks, Angel, but one more thing," I tried to catch her but she was gone. I was sure she could have told me what Simon's letters were, too. I tried back but there was no answer.

b-1-_-_-6-0-1-d. There's a word or words here and I need two more letters out of Simon's tattoo to complete it. F-8-e-d-2-d-1-e.

Give me a hand here, guys.

{16}
The Committee

DID YOU EVER have a dream in code? Last night I worked in the office at the Condo until late, trying to figure out the last two digits for the hidden code. I was so tired, I fell asleep in front of the screen. All night long I dreamed long series of random numbers and letters. Don't go thinking I solved the problem in my sleep. My head was apparently not satisfied with hexadecimal code. The dream included every letter of the alphabet and several figures from Aramaic, Chinese, and Farsi. No bolt of lightning breakthrough.

———|—|—|—|+|+|+|||||||||+|+|+|—|———

Pick a number

I WOKE UP as tired as when I fell asleep, still in the chair at the desk. When I saw what time it was, I scrambled around to make sure my makeup and hair were in place before Davy got there. There would be a party tonight but he might be ticked if he just found out Angel was gone. I don't think she told him she was going. She won't be at the party tonight and I had one of those creepy feelings that I shouldn't be here either.

When I got back to the desk, a flag I'd set up on Brenda's accounts was chiming gently. She used a credit card in the name of Ashley Lark, one of the aliases I'd recorded. It was charged yesterday in Belize. It's time I left the country. I used my James Whitcomb identity to buy a ticket on the most direct flight I could to Belize City, via Dallas/Fort Worth. At 11:55 tonight, I'm going after the bitch.

Now, back to my other problem. What are the last two characters to the code? I opened Excel and made a worksheet of the possibilities. If I can decipher what perverted word Simon thought up, I can fill in the last two numbers. But for most of the known numbers there were more than a single letter that could be substituted. 'B' could mean b, be, bee. '1' could be one, won, i, or L. '6' was just a six or a G. '0', I hate that one. O, naught, zip, zilch, aught, nada or just zero. '1' again. 'D' could be de, de-, ed (on Brenda's tattoo, Simon used just a 'd' instead of 'ed' to make elated but on his own, he used both the 'e' and the 'd' to make fated.)

Then there were all the letters in Simon's tattoo since I didn't know which two were in red. 'F' has to just be f. '8' could be eight, ate, 8. 'E', long or short sound. '2' is another goody. Two, to, too, Z, 2. I still had two 'd's, a '1', and another 'e'.

What do I know about Simon? He's a gamer and consistent. He has rules he follows or else he has to cheat. Simon loves the game too much to cheat. So, the letters should be in the order they'll be used. Angel says he can make a dirty joke out of anything. He loves money. He's obsessed with death, having used 'die' twice already. Combined with the b1, what do I have?

Bif? Bize (busy?), bile, bide, bl8d (belated), bled, blez, blei, bige (big ego?), blie.

Bi-lego-id, big-ego-id, bi-leg-old, bizesixoid (bisexual?), bi-f8-gold.

Gold! That's Simon-talk. Busy gold would work. Belated gold. Bled gold. Yes! Morbidity with the bleeding and money with the gold. I was getting impatient. What will it hurt if I try? I can always rebuild the system again if he decides to erase everything.

———|—|—|—|—||||||||||—|—|—|—|———

Gotta run now

I'M SCARED.

Davy started banging around in the living room shouting at caterers and decorators for the party tonight. The party is for the board of directors of Bio-Research Technologies, one of the hottest new stocks on the

Seattle market. But it's not Davy I'm worried about, or even the CEO of Bio-Research by himself.

I got into the thumb drive.

When I brought the computer out of hibernation, the message was still flashing on the screen: "Simon says, enter the next encryption code."

Here goes. B-1-e-d-6-0-1-d. Bled Gold. Who is bleeding, Simon?

The screen blanked and I was poised to yank the thumb drive out of the port when a message appeared on the screen.

"There's only one person in a billion who could get here, so congratulations, Dag. Everything you need is here. Simon says, 'Nail the bastards.' I'm counting on you, old friend.

The screen dissolved and was replaced with a directory of hundreds of files. I scanned through a few of them. There were bank records, commerce records, spreadsheets, email, and documents setting up offshore accounts. Dag told me he'd moved nearly two billion in assets for Simon before he died. These records showed traffic an order of magnitude greater than that.

There was a new area of fraud alive in the world, more profitable than drug traffic. I was holding one in my hand—a cellular phone.

I would have been more comfortable if I'd found some big crime syndicate in this mess. What scared me was it was controlled by eight men and one woman. The Committee comprised senior officers of every major corporation in the Northwest. And the way they were working would evade detection by the most careful auditors. They weren't defrauding their own companies. They were preying on each other's.

These were the kind of people who could buy and sell a dozen of me a minute and not even care where I ended up. And one of them would be a guest at the Condo this evening. No wonder Angel had run. I'm doing the same.

I packaged up a compressed file of everything on the thumb drive and sent it to Jordan with instructions on how to access the data.

Then I packed.

———————+++++++++++++++++++++++++———————

THE PARTY STARTED at seven. I'd planned my escape route but people started getting there before I was prepared. Now I'd have to watch for a break and make a run for it. Of course, the first one to arrive would have to be Cinnamon.

She checked her phone and purse at the door and headed directly for the private room opposite the office.

I'm sure she knew there were cameras all over the Condo. Probably knew where each one was. She went into the dressing room area and leaned into the mirror to powder her nose. She was wearing an elegant pale blue gown that accented her tawny skin tones. It was a scoop neck front but the back was cut so low it nearly showed her butt crack.

She turned so she was facing the camera and I saw the tube of lipstick drop to the floor. That was when I realized she was putting on a show. She tapped her foot angrily, made a big deal out of seeing where the tube landed, and bent over to retrieve it. While she was bent over, the straps of her gown slid down her shoulders and when she straightened up, the dress slipped down to her waist leaving her pert little breasts exposed to the camera. Again, she made a little display about being silly enough to let her dress fall off and slowly slid the straps up her shoulders. She finished tidying herself up and turned to leave the private room. Just as she pulled the door open, she glanced up at the camera and blew a little kiss to it.

The girl had been giving James Whitcomb a show, intentionally inviting me to call for her. She was going to be so disappointed when she found out I was a girl and we'd both be embarrassed when she found out which girl. I suddenly understood the impulse guys have to run when a girl shows interest in them. I was about to run.

The party was moving along by then. Davy served drinks and monitored the door. He checked everyone through and made sure the house rules were followed. No phones, cameras, or weapons. I think our Condo security was better than an airport. I watched the CEO hand out gifts to his employees in the living room and I thought I could make it to the service elevator behind the kitchen when there was a knock at my door. I checked the monitors and Cinnamon was standing outside looking up at the camera. She tilted her head and waved her fingers at the camera.

Now what was I going to do? I could pretend not to be here, but then she would go ask Davy and there would be too much attention drawn to me. A flash of lightning and boom of thunder outside the windows shocked me as a gust of wind blew the cover off the hot tub. I needed to leave. When I opened the door, Cinnamon rushed in and wrapped me in a warm embrace, searching for my lips with hers.

"James," she breathed in my face as she kissed my cheek. Before she could reach my lips, I regained control.

"Cinnamon, baby," I husked as I pulled her away.

"Have you recovered from your jetlag? I hope so."

"I'm fine, Cinnamon, but I'm getting ready to leave. I have to leave on a trip tonight." My mind was in overdrive, trying to think of a way to use Cinnamon to get me out of the penthouse suite. Another gust of wind toppled a potted plant on the patio. A real storm was blowing in. Those plants are heavy.

"Take me with you, James," she whispered. "I'll be anything you'd like me to be. I'll make your trip so much more enjoyable."

"I don't doubt you would, Cinnamon," I said. "But I need to get out of here now and I'd like you to help me. I don't want to be recognized by any of the guys out there. They don't know I'm here. I'm doing a little audit of their activities, you know."

"Oh, I won't tell anyone, James. I promise." Just then the phone on the desk rang. I knew it had rung in the bar as well and a quick glance at the monitor showed Davy answering it. I reached over and flicked on the speaker phone and pressed mute so I could hear and not be heard.

"Everything is going fine, Ms. B," Davy said. "Mr. J got here on Tuesday and put everything in shape right away."

"Who is Mr. J?" I heard Brenda's voice over a slightly delayed long distance connection. I wished I knew where she was calling from but this conversation was getting dangerous already.

"The guy you sent to take control," Davy said. "He's got a lease signed by you and everything. Said he was part of the Committee."

"There is no Mr. J on the Committee, Davy. You've been infiltrated."

"Shit." Davy hung up the phone and headed straight to the CEO of Bio-Research. This looked bad. I glanced up and Cinnamon was looking at me in horror.

"I'm sorry, Cinnamon. I'm one of the good guys," I said. I played the one card I thought would save me. "Dag sent me. Are you with me?"

I grabbed my bag and headed for the door, seeing the CEO had just looked up at the camera.

Then everything went black. It was a little pop and the monitors went out, the lights went out, and the locks all closed. Another blast of wind hit the side of the building and rattled the glass so hard I thought it would cave in. I could hear the screams out in the Condo and a gasp of breath from Cinnamon as she clutched my arm. I opened the door and pushed her toward the poolroom, letting the door latch behind me. It's one thing to get out of an electronically locked door. You just turn the handle and leave. But I was counting on the lock delaying any pursuit.

We emerged from the poolroom into the buffeting wind. I used the wind to help me topple another plant in front of the door. I'd never seen a storm like this in Seattle. Downtown was dark. Power was out everywhere. Clutching Cinnamon to me against the cold, we were almost blown over when we were hit by the wind. Climbing the ladder to the rooftop access stair didn't seem like as good an idea as it had in the office. I could hear someone crashing into the poolroom door but the plant effectively blocked it. Flashlights started coming on in the living room. We had no choice.

I stripped off my jacket and wrapped it around Cinnamon, yelling for her to stay low as we crossed the patio to the ladder. The downed plant by the hot tub proved a challenge for Cinnamon to get over in her gown. I picked her up and set her on the bottom step of the ladder, following her closely and using my body to hold her against the ladder. She hit the roof and rolled as another gust of wind hit. I was afraid she was going over the edge.

I grabbed her leg and dragged her back, staying low on the roof and crawling toward the door. I was just reaching for the latch when Davy came blasting through the door.

Use greater force against itself. I quickly sidestepped and gave Davy a gentle shove with my foot. He went sailing straight ahead and over the edge of the roof. Cinnamon screamed as I heard a splash below and shoved her through the open door. Davy had gone into the hot tub. I was satisfied he was no longer a threat. I half dragged, half carried Cinnamon down the stairs all the way to the garage and my car. I ripped the canvas off and stuffed it in the back seat along with my bag and we tore out of the garage, breaking the gate off since it wouldn't rise in the blackout.

I turned right and hit Second southbound, dodging around cars confused by the blackout. Sirens were going off all over town as police tried to attend to the most urgent traffic conditions. I just barreled through the intersections with my lights flashing dim and bright like an emergency vehicle. Cinnamon whimpered in her seat as I turned on traffic radio to see what the best route would be. Instead of heading for the freeway, I connected to 99 south and headed for the airport. I wasn't going to enjoy taking off in this wind.

Finally, Cinnamon spoke.

"Who are you, really?" she asked. "Are you with the FBI? I'll tell you everything I know. I promise."

"I'm counting on that, Cinnamon," I said.

"How did you know my name?" she asked. "The first night I saw you, you called me by name but I'd never told you. I don't know why I didn't think of that before. Who are you?"

"I'm a friend and you are about to become my new partner," I said. "But first, you have to promise me not to overreact to what I'm going to say. Got your seatbelt fastened?" I asked.

"Yes," she said, literally checking her belt.

"I'm a friend," I repeated, softening my voice. As I proceeded to describe our first real meeting at the Palomino Grill weeks ago, I continued to soften my voice until I'd reached my normal tones.

"Debbie?" she gasped.

"Cinnamon," I said, returning to my most masculine tone, "don't ever call me Debbie."

"But, Deb. I… We… You… Then…"

"I'm sorry, Cinnamon," I said. "I didn't want to lead you on but I did tell you that I could disguise myself in such a way you'd never tell who I was. We had a bet, remember?"

"Yeah. Oh, Deb. What I said. Or suggested."

"Forget about it. You didn't know I was a girl."

"Well, it doesn't make that much difference to me," she said, reaching out to put a hand on my leg. "I like it both ways." Now I was dumbstruck.

"Um, well… Look… I mean…" I wasn't handling this as well as she was.

"Where are we going, Deb?" she asked.

"The airport," I said. "I'd like you to drop me off and take care of the car. If you don't feel safe going back to your own apartment, I've got a safe place for you to stay. I'm going to need someone to monitor things for me back at my office. What do you think? Would you like to do some work for me?"

"I think I just quit my day job," she said. "Deb, I'd do anything for you. But can't I go on the trip with you?"

"No, honey. Seattle might not be the safest place in the world but where I'm headed is even less safe."

"Where is that?"

"I'm going after Ms. B."

"Deb! You can't do that! Let's just go away someplace and wait till this whole thing blows over."

"It's not going to blow over, Cinnamon," I said. "I just sent info to FinCEN that will put some of Seattle's biggest executives behind bars if they can sort out the data. The only person on the Committee who's missing is Ms. B. I'm going to bring her in, dead or alive."

Cinnamon was quiet for a few minutes and I was afraid I'd completely overwhelmed her. In some ways, she was more vulnerable than I was.

"That's why Angel took off yesterday, isn't it?"

"You knew she was gone?"

We pulled into the departure lane at SeaTac. There were still lights but it was blowing up an incredible storm. This just wasn't going to be fun. I gave Cinnamon my keys, including office and both apartments. She gave me back my jacket and I pulled a sweatshirt out of the emergency pack in the back seat to keep her warm. Then I grabbed my bag and walked around the front of the car.

"Thanks, Cinnamon," I said as we met. She didn't say anything. She just wrapped her arms around me and gave me another big kiss. I didn't resist too much. I wanted to look like just another businessman heading out on a business trip. And she sure can kiss.

———— +-++++++IIIIIIII++++-+- ————

Now I'm AT the airport waiting. All flights were cancelled or delayed because of the storm. I'll sit here in the executive lounge and hope no one else on the Committee decides to take a late-night trip.

And think about Cinnamon's kiss.

{17}
Flight

W E DIDN'T GET OFF THE GROUND until 4:00 a.m. and that was a miracle. The lights at SeaTac had flickered a few times and winds smashed into everything. An hour out of Seattle, the pilot announced over a million people in Seattle were without power and we'd been one of the last flights to leave SeaTac, which was now closed and without power. Taking off was like riding a rollercoaster, only not as much fun.

---

where the action is

MY ORIGINAL SCHEDULE showed a seven-hour layover at DFW but since our flight was five hours late, I had spent most of the layover time in Seattle. I'd managed to stay plugged in so I had a full battery in the little laptop and as long as I was on the ground, I had access to my VPN. The late takeoff gave me plenty of time to dig deeper into what was going on in Belize. Not only is Brenda there, she's spending a bunch of money at local markets in San Pedro. It looks like she's settling in for a long winter's nap.

The emergency UPS system in the vault kept one server running out of the ten Dag set up. At least I can still do research.

So, Brenda owns property under the name of Ashley Lark in San Pedro. I booked a reservation at the Belize Yacht Club, even though I had to commit to a week's stay at $165 a night. I also had to book a fifteen-minute flight on a local carrier to get from the airport in Belize City to Ambergris Caye. Typical of Brenda to choose the most touristy party of Belize.

I checked my voice mail remotely to see if any message came in from Jordan. Cinnamon had called from my apartment. She said the power was only out for a flicker on Capitol Hill, so I have power and she's staying in my apartment. She planned to email work and resign since her CEO is also one of the members of the Committee. She planned to stay in my place until I call. I'll do that after I'm settled in San Pedro.

I keep going back to the list of people who make up the Committee. I can't believe some of these guys would stoop so low. They each have a shell company selling mobile phone services. One of the other companies subscribes to their service for the company phones. The shell company contracts to buy network time from the actual mobile operator at a base amount. Then they route the calls through privately owned carriers that mark up the rates. Those carriers bill the service back to the mobile operator at an inflated cost. The mobile operator is getting five or ten cents a minute for calls and are being billed a dollar or a dollar-fifty. The big gouge is into the pocket of the operator but the shell companies are selling at a huge profit, as well. As a result, each company's cellular bill is higher than if they just worked out an arrangement with the mobile operator directly.

These guys have sold services, not only to each other, but to eighty percent of the top 500 companies in the world. They're raking in billions.

Time to board for Belize.

Beach time
BEAUTIFUL!

I wish I was here for pleasure. It was eighty-five degrees when I landed and now that the sun has set, it is a perfect 72. My room on the second floor looks out over the water with a perfectly wonderful lanai where I can sit and have coffee in the morning. It's paradise.

I landed right on time at three-thirty this afternoon and caught the shuttle flight to Ambergris Caye, the largest of the islands off the coast of Belize and just inside the Barrier Reef. The sand is perfectly white and so is the hotel. The room is spacious and comfortable. People are running all over everyplace waiting on you.

Once I was settled in, I did some shopping. I hadn't packed for this kind of adventure but I did toss in extra wigs and my makeup kit. I bought a bikini (much to the surprise of the shop clerk until I told her it was for my girlfriend), a pareu, and sandals. When I got back to my room, I stripped off all my makeup and showered thoroughly. There's no reason for me to pretend to be a boy here. Even if Jordan didn't revoke the warrant for my arrest, he can't enforce it here and he can't stop me from traveling elsewhere.

On the other hand, Brenda knows me only as a blonde, which is why I also grabbed my short red bob when I was abandoning my apartment last weekend. It's an easy look and with makeup that plays down my lips and cheekbones, I don't look anything like I did when Brenda met me in Dag's office. I'm now Riley Finn. I went to the hotel desk and told them my boyfriend instructed me to register with him and they took down my passport information. Now I could keep James Whitcomb hidden for a while.

I had a nice meal. It's been so long since I actually relaxed and had a meal that I indulged myself at the Celebrity Restaurant. I had the BBQ Grill Chicken, Vegetables, Rice & Beans, and Chocolate Cake. It was all exquisite, even if a little pricey. I'm trying to figure out who I'm going to bill these expenses to. I might have to tap into Brenda's bank accounts!

As I was leaving a man approached me and offered to buy me a nightcap at the Splash! Poolside bar. I was about to blow him off—he was old enough to be my grandfather. Then I realized it was Jonathan Reinholdt, CEO of Bio-Research Technologies. I'd just seen him at the Condo! I let him down a little more gently and suggested we take a rain check until tomorrow evening.

Reinholdt is one of the Committee. He's staying here at the Yacht Club. I'm betting his wife isn't here. I guess it's time to go back to work.

Casing the joint

IT WAS A morning for some serious shopping. The only girl clothes I had were the bikini and sarong I bought yesterday. That was adequate dress for most venues on the island but I didn't want to be known for one outfit the entire time I was here. Saturday morning markets gave me everything I needed. The boutiques filled in the need for a decent dress in a gay print and I got a lot of accessories. It's a little slinky but most of the clothes I saw don't cover much. I plan to pump Mr. Reinholdt for information. He could be my ticket into Ashley Lark's home. It would be a lot easier if I was invited in instead of breaking in. You can't tell me Jonathan Reinholdt is on the island for any reason other than to visit Ms. Lark.

Remind me not to call him Mr. Reinholdt this evening. He hasn't told me his name yet and god knows he might have an alias here, too.

I'm lathering myself up with sunblock and dressed in khaki shorts and a lightweight white shirt. I've been keeping the scar on my right side covered as much as possible. I'm planning on a little hike this afternoon.

———————————————————

THE PLACE IS like a fortress except it doesn't have a drawbridge. I don't think the bridge draws up, at least. It crosses a tiny stream one could easily skip across if the bridge was raised. There's a guard at the gate and another strolling the grounds on the beach side. That one stopped me when I crossed the stream down by the ocean. He just warned me that I couldn't go above the tide line. The shore itself is public.

A huge yacht is anchored about a quarter mile offshore. Either it's Brenda's (which would explain how she got down here from Mexico without triggering an immigration alert) or it's another visitor.

When Davy told me there was no meeting of the Committee at the Condo, I finally figured out they had to meet elsewhere. The whole Committee wouldn't risk being seen together in one place in Seattle unless it was at some charitable event. Their companies have a reputation of being fierce competitors with each other. No one would raise an eyebrow at them all traveling south for R&R right before Christmas. Next week would probably find them scattered at various ski resorts.

If you added up the entire net worth of everyone in Seattle, more than half of it would be in the hands of these eight men. And that's only the legitimate part Forbes reports on. It doesn't include any of the hidden funds in Swiss bank accounts or offshore banks that aren't required to report to the US Government.

It strikes me as odd they'd wrap up all their illicit dealings in one industry, though. I need to do more research on that.

I'm meeting Mr. Wrong for dinner at eight, so I'd better get made up and slip into the slinky dress. Wish me luck.

{18}
Dinner with the enemy

I WILL GO TO HELL FOR THIS. If I'm lucky, I'll be dead first.

Angel told me, back in November when I was trying to get a feel for what the condo business was all about, the objective was never to sell sex to an old fart. It was to sell the idea that sex wasn't beyond the realm possibility. And to make him pay for the dream rather than a reality.

It's not as easy as it sounds.

Selling the dream

I MET MR. Reinholdt in the hotel lobby and he introduced himself as Jon Rentz. Not very imaginative but then, look at the name I'm using. There's no Riley Finn to complain about me using his name outside the world of *Buffy the Vampire Slayer*. I chose it because all my aliases have something to do with Riley.

So, there we were, two impostors having a lovely polite but flirtatious dinner together beside the pool in an 80-degree paradise with the most spectacular night sky above I'd ever seen. There are several people I can think of, living and dead, I'd rather share this experience with.

I wasn't at all hesitant to order the 'grill marinated lobster tail with rice and sauce vegetables' at $65, nor to have my fill of single origin dark chocolates with coffee for dessert. Mr. Rentz, however, seemed somewhat disappointed when he offered me a glass of Chenin Blanc ($120 per bottle) from a Northern California vineyard that would have cost $12 at Fred Meyer. Of course, the menu I had didn't have prices on it, but I looked last night when I ate alone. The Dom here is $750 a bottle. Unbelievable.

"So, Miss Finn," he said, "from where do you hail?" *He's as pretentious as the menu.*

"Chatham, Mass," I answered. "How about you?"

"Seattle," he answered. *I told you he wasn't creative.* Fake name but he's living in the same place. I doubt he even used a fake passport to travel.

"Does it really rain there all the time?" I asked.

"No," he said, "we just tell people that to keep the population down. If everyone knew how beautiful our city is, we'd never keep them out."

"Ah. Like an exclusive club, huh?" *Probe.*

"You might say so. Finn. What nationality is that?"

"My father claimed to be full Irish, though it was his grandfather who immigrated to the US in the 1800s. He said that's where I get my red hair. And my temper," I laughed.

"And the blue eyes?" *Oops!* I usually wear green contacts with this wig but I didn't bring those with me.

"My mother is as Swedish as they come," I said. "She's tall and blonde and blue-eyed. I don't know why I couldn't have gotten her hair as well as her eyes."

"You'd look good as a blonde," he said. "You should try it. They say blondes have more fun."

"Oh, hair color never stopped me from having fun," I said. "What do you do in Seattle, Mr. Rentz?" It was time to move the conversation of my fake identity and see what I could get out of him.

"I manage a little pharmaceutical company. Seattle is very big in bio-tech." *Really no imagination.* I bet he doesn't know what other businesses are in Seattle outside those owned by his cohort.

"That sounds very exciting. Are you finding a cure for cancer or AIDS?" 'Where's your social conscience?' is what I was saying.

"That's a tough problem, better left to people smarter than I am. I just sell what they develop." *What?* Was that a hint of false humility I detected? He didn't add 'at grossly overpriced profit margins.'

"You must sell a lot of it to vacation down here in Belize. I had to save a year for this little trip. This is a vacation, isn't it? Or are you selling drugs?" I whispered.

"Mostly… Let's say a working vacation. I have a business meeting to attend Monday but other than that, it is a lovely place to spend Christmas."

"It's such a shame you are here alone," I said. "Don't you have family to spend the holiday with?"

"Well, my wife will be joining me Wednesday after the meetings are over. She doesn't really like it down here that much." He dropped his voice conspiratorially. "We have three days to enjoy ourselves before she gets here." *The cheating cad.*

"Oh, I can't enjoy myself too much. I'm here with my boyfriend." *Let's see how you handle that, lech.*

"Where is your boyfriend now that he lets you wander unescorted where any manner of ne'er-do-well could attach to you?"

"He got hit with a stomach bug the minute we landed. He's absolutely no fun to be with when he's running to the bathroom every ten minutes. I'm sure you'll see him around by the time your wife gets here, though," I said. *Will you pay for my company with a little information.* "What kind of business meeting gets held on an island in Central America?" I asked. "When you say pharmaceuticals, you don't mean you're a drug runner, do you?"

"I sell drugs," he answered. "But they are all legal drugs. Some with a better profit margin when imported from facilities where labor is cheaper. In the US, there are certain restraints on what people can discuss in a meeting if they are in the same business. We have to discuss these things as we share many of the same suppliers. We'd never get anywhere with our businesses if one manufacturer was selling a product at a significantly reduced rate. It's a matter of self-regulating the trade, so to speak." *Price fixing.*

Okay. He's a bigger idiot than I thought. Who the hell covers up an illegal meeting by inventing a different kind of illegal meeting? Or maybe he *is* meeting others in the pharmaceutical industry as well. And maybe he isn't an idiot but is just flat-out so arrogant that he believes he's immune to consequences. He might actually be telling me that he's meeting people to divide up the market or fix the price of aspirin around the world. Why? Because he simply can't believe anyone in the world could be smart enough to understand what was going on. He's probably right. Who'd believe little old me if I launched a story about a secret meeting in Belize that would result in a 500 percent increase in the cost of an EpiPen?

By the time he started trying to push a glass of cognac on me, I'd pretty much had enough. By a stroke of good fortune, that's when Prince Charming arrived.

He was a nice sex feet tall—I mean six feet—dark hair cropped close, trim and fit, and about thirty years old. I was looking forward to meeting him on the beach sometime soon. I bet he looks great in his swim trunks.

"Jon, fancy meeting you here," he said, striding up to my dinner date with an outstretched hand. Mr. Rentz rose reluctantly and accepted the greeting.

"Hawkins. The surprise is mutual. What brings you here?" He was just a little tetchy.

"Obviously, the same thing as you. I've heard how magnificent the women are down here. I see you've already reeled one in, eh?" He turned to me and smiled the most brilliant perfect smile I've ever seen. I melted just a little. He held out his hand.

"I'm Ray Hawkins, Miss. If you wear out the old guy, look me up."

"Thank you," I said, taking his hand. I was contemplating taking it home with me. Him attached, of course. "Riley Finn."

"Nice to meet you, Miss Finn. I certainly hope to see more of you." *Yes, yes. Much more of me. Okay! OMG! He's beautiful.* "I'll see you around, Jon. Maybe we can go out for some deep-sea fishing."

"Sure, sure. We'll make an arrangement later. Good evening."

Ray Hawkins took his beautiful body to the bar. Mr. Rentz ordered another cognac.

"Young ass," Mr. Rentz said confidentially across the table. "He thinks those video games he sells are real. Let me give you some advice, Miss Finn. Stay away from him. He's a user. Reputation for going through beautiful women like water. Wouldn't have him in my club, I'll tell you that, for sure."

Suddenly, the conversation took an interesting turn. My dear Mr. Rentz became a fatherly sage. The presence of a man about half his age must have struck his ego much harder than I imagined. The more glasses of cognac Mr. Rentz drank while I put away $8 glasses of Perrier, the more fatherly and protective he became. He leaned across the table and patted my hand, whispering deep secrets about how men behave when in the presence of beautiful women.

"I see it all the time," he said. "Hell, when I was that age, I was the same way. You see, Miss Finn—may I call you Riley?" *I think he's paid enough for that privilege.* I nodded. "Young men only see a woman's beauty. They don't understand what a great contribution women make to society, business, science, or even politics. Older men, like myself—I don't kid myself about my age; I'm old enough to be your grandfather—older men see the potential for a smart woman to make a real impact on the world. What we really want to do is help her realize her potential. For example, what do you do, Riley? What is your profession?"

"I'm a customer engineer for a manufacturer of precision instrumentation. I'm responsible for making sure their installations are properly set up, their employees are trained, and that they never have a problem with our products." Thank you, Lars for insisting that when we create a persona for an alias, we do a complete background on where we are supposed to work, even what color our house is.

"You see!" he exclaimed. "You see what I mean?" He drank down another cognac. He seemed to have forgotten I wasn't drinking and poured two more. In the next few minutes, he drank both of them. "I knew the minute I saw you, you weren't just a pretty face. You have real talent and promise. If you were in Seattle, I could arrange for you to meet people who could help your career. As your sponsor, I could get you a job with one of the big companies. Not just a field job, but something to allow you to develop your management potential. I've a young woman working in my company who has that kind of potential as a senior marketing manager. She was introduced to me by one of my associates. We are always on the lookout for smart beautiful young women."

Ding-ding! Bells went off in my head. My dear little Cinnamon happens, in her real life, to be a marketing manager for a pharmaceutical company. Was. Apparently, Rentz didn't know she'd just resigned. In short, Mr. Rentz was leading up to an offer to come join the women of the Condo. If only he knew how I'd just escaped from the Condo. But the invitation wasn't forthcoming tonight. Mr. Rentz was now seriously into his drinking. I'd seen it with my mother a hundred times. Once they get to a certain point, the booze is the most important thing, not the people you are with. It made me sick.

I didn't show it. I didn't show how much I loathed him, his drinking, or his insinuations. I didn't show my intention to bury him and the other seven men on the Committee.

I actually supported him all the way to his room—excuse me, suite—with another bottle of cognac and managed to extract myself at the door with many sincere thanks for all the advice he'd given me and an excuse that I needed to see how my sick boyfriend was doing.

I glanced over my shoulder as we left and noticed the handsome Mr. Hawkins watching us leave.

{19}
Lying low

I DIDN'T LIKE what I saw at brunch Sunday morning and hustled myself back to my room. It looks like the full Committee is meeting. Stan Metzger of the PNW Publishing Group walked in beside René Fortier, the founder of one of the largest Internet services groups in the country. I was shocked to see the CEO of Allied Cellular with them.

———+—+—+—+++++++++—+—+—+———

Personal Assistant

I RAN TO my room and called Cinnamon. I'd had to buy an International SIM when I landed, so, of course, she had no idea who was calling. She still answered on first ring, sounding a little panicked.

"Hello? Who is this?"

"It's me, Deb. Are you okay?"

"Oh, thank God! I've been so worried," she said. "Where are you?"

"I'm fine. I've been really lucky. How are you?"

"Seattle is a mess. Downtown is fine and so is your apartment. Parts of town are still without power and the East Side is a virtual blackout. According to the news there are still 700,000 customers without power."

"Good Lord! I need you to go down and check my office."

"I did. Am. I'm there now. I'm sorry, Deb. It's a real mess."

"Still no power?"

"Oh, you've got power, all right," she answered, "but the place has been ransacked. When I say a mess, I mean everything is torn up. Someone came in and vandalized it during the storm. A window was broken and there's water damage. I got a glass company to come in and do an emergency repair on the window this morning."

"You're terrific, Cinnamon. Please be sure Maizie's bed is cleaned up. I don't want the poor girl to lie on any glass."

"Deb? There's no glass in the room. The window was broken from inside. I was only in here once, after Dag's memorial, but I'm sure there's a chair missing. It's probably in the Sound."

"I need you to give me a verbal survey of the room," I said, panic just at bay. "Stand in the middle of the office and start facing the window. Describe the damage as you turn to your left."

"Sure. The window has been repaired. The sofa is hacked to ribbons, cushions on the floor. Maizie's bed is pretty much shredded. There's an overturned pedestal table with a vase broken on the floor. Then, through the door to the outer office…"

"Wait," I said. "What about the television mounted on the wall?"

"There's no television. Oh, I see. There's a wire cut off and hanging out of the wall. It looks like they took the screen. Sorry."

"Okay," I answered. "You're at the door into the office. Continue." I held my breath.

"The outer office is in the same condition. Desk drawers have been pulled out and emptied. The file cabinet is trashed. I can see through the bathroom door that the shelves have been torn out of the medicine cabinet. Back in this room, desk drawers are lying on the floor with contents dumped out. Books have all been stripped off the shelves. The desk is turned on edge. There's another pedestal table near the wall and a painting has been slashed open and torn off the wall. The curtains were pulled down from the windows. A recliner chair, also cut to shreds. I'm sure there was another chair near the window that isn't here. And the coffee table is upside down. I'm sorry, Deb. It's really a mess. I got the window replaced but have just been taking pictures of everything else so you can file an insurance claim. Do you want me to call the police? I don't have anything that would tell them I work for you and I couldn't get hold of you when I tried earlier."

I breathed. Cinnamon couldn't have missed another room behind the desk with shelves for computer servers. The vault was still secure.

"It sounds like I'm going to have to pretty much start over." A tear was leaking out of my eye. Everything that was Dag's was destroyed. Even Maizie's bed. "I'll need you to call Jordan Grant. He'll come over to investigate. Thank you for getting the window repaired."

"Wait till you see the bill."

"I'll bet they gouged me on that one," I said. "I'm going to want to go through everything that's left both to reclaim our files and to see if I can identify anything missing. I guess you don't need to come back to the office."

"I'll make sure everything is kept for you, Deb," Cinnamon said softly. "But I'm not going to let you come back to this mess. Is there anything here you especially don't want me to look at? I'll try not to be nosy while I'm cleaning."

"Really, Cinnamon. You don't have to do that."

"You hired me, remember?"

"Yeah. Are you sure you want to work for me? It can get kind of dangerous."

"Pharmaceuticals were getting kind of boring," she said. "I sent in my resignation Friday."

"Cinnamon, did your boss know you were there Thursday night?"

"No. I wasn't supposed to be there. I hid out until I thought it was safe to come and see you. The girls aren't supposed to be at a party with a group they work with. You know what I mean? It's something about a law called 'quid pro quo.' Responsibilities as a hostess in the Condo never cross with your responsibilities in your day job."

"But your CEO was there Thursday night," I said. "Can you tell me anything about him?"

"Mostly, he's a really nice man. I never even met him the first year I was with Bio-Research. He sent me a congratulations letter when I got promoted to Senior Marketing Manager. That's what bugs me, Deb. The members of the Committee all seem like really nice guys. I don't know all of them, but the ones I've met have been the least likely to, you know, want to have sex with you on the sofa. They all have their minds somewhere else."

"Yeah. On money," I said absently. *That might mean I won't have as much trouble with Mr. Rentz as I was afraid.* "Tell me about Mr. Reinholdt's family."

"He has a nice wife who looks like she came out of a Pillsbury cookbook, if you know what I mean," she giggled. "I think three grown children. That's really all the personal information I know about him."

"Cinnamon, you'll have to get more curious about things if you work for me," I laughed. "Seriously, you should go back to work for Bio-Research. I can't pay you anything like what they can."

"I don't need that much money, Deb," she answered. "I've been careful saving up from my salary, 401k, and tips. That's one of the things we were taught when we went to the Condo. If any of us were found to be using drugs or spending too freely, we were cut off and not allowed back. We're all pretty clean-cut. But I don't want to be a pharmaceuticals marketing manager. It's what they said I was best suited for. It's boring. Your work isn't boring, Deb. I told you Thursday night, I'll be anything you want me to be for you."

"Honey, don't pin too many hopes on anything personal happening. Quid pro quo laws apply to our relationship as employer and employee, just like they do at Bio-Research. And as much as I like you, I'm not gay, or really even bi. I just don't happen to be very lucky with men."

"Tell me about it, sister," she sighed. "Well, unless you are firing me, I think I'll call Jordan Grant and start cleaning up this mess."

"You're a treasure, Cinnamon," I said. "Be careful."

Geez. I'm sure Dag gave me that lecture at least a dozen times. And look how I behaved. What have I gotten myself into?

Surveillance

I HAVE LIMITED resources here. I can't depend on gadgets other than my laptop and my cell phone. But I've got eyes and ears and I intend to find out what is going on at that meeting this week.

I put on my khaki shorts and headed up the beach with a pair of cheap binoculars I bought at a kiosk on the beach. Brenda's house sits on a couple of acres of beachfront about two miles north of San Pedro. You can get there via a sandy road that comes in at the little bridge and security gate, or by water and the beach. A security guard patrols the beach and makes sure that walkers keep moving and don't pause on Brenda's 200' of beachfront. I passed the guard and waved to him. I figure if he gets used to seeing me, he'll pay less attention to me. As soon as I passed Brenda's property, I cut up from the beach onto the property next door. Another tropical mansion is under construction with a 1.5 million-dollar price tag. I thought at first it was three million, but the Belize dollar is two to one against the American dollar. I decided to investigate the new construction. Being Sunday, no workers were around and I walked right in. On the second floor I found a window overlooking Brenda's property.

I tried snapping a picture with my cellphone. Maybe with computer enhancement I could get enough detail to record the Committee arriving at the meeting from up here. I'd identified a dining room and a bedroom from my perch. I could add a picture to the evidence I'd sent Jordan. I wondered why he hadn't moved to stop the Committee from coming down to Belize but maybe he was just being extra careful to have an airtight case. That was his problem.

"If you try the attic window you can see the pool area and the living room patio," a voice said behind me. I nearly fell out the window. The guy had come up so quietly behind me, he caught me completely by surprise. I spun, ready to defend myself, and was face to uncomfortably close face with Prince Charming. I mean Ray Hawkins.

"I was just…" I stammered.

"Just trying to get an exclusive story," he said. "I can well imagine. Good job figuring out where they were going to meet. Did Jon tell you?"

"No, I… well, yes, I guess so." I wasn't sure what to do with this but from his perspective he'd given me a perfect cover. I could be a reporter on a story. "Don't tell me you're going to try to scoop me on this," I said.

"No, no. I'm here purely for corporate espionage. When wealthy men who wield a lot of power get together, those of us who are left out want to know what they are talking about."

"If I hear anything, I'll let you know," I said, squeezing past him and heading for the stair.

"I'd appreciate that," he said. "You know, you might get a lot closer if you stick with Jon… What name did he give you?"

"Rentz."

"Right. Stick with Jon Rentz. I'll bet he invites you along. He's always been a sucker for a beautiful face. And body."

"Thanks a lot," I said curtly. "If you aren't asking me out, I guess I have nothing better to do with my time."

"I never tread on another man's soil," he said. "Not without an invitation."

"Mine's not coming and his doesn't count," I said. "Just so you know."

I stormed down the stairs and out the front gates, walking back to San Pedro along the sandy road that fronted the property. Hawkins had a point. I knew all the men on the Committee liked to have pretty girls on their arms when they got together. Maybe I should play up to Mr. Rentz and see if he'll invite me.

I was still musing about that when I got back to the Beach Club and the man in question stopped me in the lobby.

"Miss Finn," he said. I turned toward him. "Riley, I hope you will indulge me with your presence at dinner again tonight. That is, if your boyfriend is still under the weather."

"Mr. Rentz, how delightful," I answered. "Shall I join you in the Celebrity Restaurant?"

"No, no. I had something more islandy in mind. Meet me down here at seven-thirty in beach wear and we'll go to Elvi's for a real Island meal." *Beach wear? You lech. Okay. Kindly, fatherly, embezzling lech.*

"I'll see you here," I said gaily and hopped up to my room.

There was one little piece of investigation I needed to do online when I got back to my room. I looked up *Helen of Troy*. I'm not looking for a Homerian epic poem. I'm looking for the owner of the huge yacht anchored off the beach at Brenda's little island home. And I found it. A certain major sports franchise owner who likes to party at sea. I'll bet that baby is armed.

{20}
Pampered, spoiled, and searched

S O THAT'S WHAT A SPA IS ALL ABOUT? I could get used to being pampered like that. I've been soaked, sweated, massaged, oiled, manicured, pedicured, made up, and dressed up. And this gown is really something else!

———— +—+—+—+HIIIIII+—+—+—+——

Dinner on the beach

I SHOULD START at the beginning. I played my part perfectly last night. A little flirtation. A little bare skin exposed where my sarong gapped open to show my bikini. A little too much laughter at jokes that weren't that funny. Angel would be so proud of me.

And to cap the evening off, an invitation to join him for a dinner party at a mansion nearby tomorrow evening.

"This little outfit will be perfect for the late afternoon by the pool," Jon said. "You see, I am a bit vain. There's always a competition among the attendees to see who can be accompanied by the most attractive and brilliant young woman. You are my new discovery. After lounging and cocktails, we'll dress formally for dinner."

"Oh dear!" I said. "I haven't a thing formal with me."

"Miss Finn, my dear, I insist you let me buy you something. I'll take care of everything. Spend the day at the Sol Spa tomorrow. I'll make the arrangement. They'll shop for you, bring you a dress, and make sure it fits correctly. Something fitting for the party. It will be my little thank you for brightening a few days with me here in the sun. And you might even meet someone who could help advance your career. I'll make the introductions but it will be up to you to convince a potential employer of your qualifications."

"I hardly know what to say, Mr. Rentz," I gasped.

"Please, call me Jon, dear. And think nothing of it."

Whoa! It was a little more difficult to extract myself from him as he wasn't quite as loaded. But I managed without injuring him or his pride. I have to tell you: I spent a long time in the shower after I got home. *Ewww!*

When I got out of the shower, I went onto my lanai and looked out at the beach in the moonlight. How I wish I was just here enjoying myself. Down on the beach a man was talking on his cellphone, animatedly waving his arms. It must be awfully hard to hear down by the water. Some people just can't leave work behind.

Then he turned and looked up at my window. He stopped his conversation, or else he was just listening, because he stood there looking up at me and I felt like Juliet on the balcony with Romeo in the garden. Prince Ray Charming raised a hand and tentatively waved.

I waved back before slipping out of sight in my room.

Sol Spa

I HAD A heart to heart conversation with the spa manager when I showed up for my appointment at nine. She was a lovely woman and spoke impeccable English. She was a little older than the bikini-clad technicians running around the spa and, like most of the managers I'd encountered at stores and restaurants, she was not native.

"I couldn't wait to get out of dreary England and when this opportunity presented itself, I was packed and on a plane in a trice," she said. "Now tell me what has you worried about your spa treatment."

"I have recently finished treatment for cancer," I lied. "According to the doctors, it is in remission, but there have been side effects from the treatment. I'm quite bald and only wear a wig. And I'm still healing from surgery on my side." Even as part of a cover story, I blushed brightly at the confessions.

People were far more sympathetic to the story of a cancer patient who lost all her hair to chemotherapy than to a woman who was allergic to her own hair so it fell out. "I am having such a wonderful time here—a celebration of recovery—I would hate for Mr. Rentz to discover my condition. He wants my hair done for the party. Can you simply style my wig?"

"Oh, my dear!" she cried. "You poor thing. We will do everything in our power to turn you out special for your party. The truth is, we deal with a lot of women who wear wigs. Usually, they are much older than you but don't want to look it. Instead of dying and styling their own hair, they don wigs like accessories, different for every outfit. I will personally tend to the styling and I have an adhesive that will allow you to even dip in the pool without endangering its security."

"Madam Wilson, your help is so appreciated."

And that started the most attention my body has had since the doctors stitched my side. Once into the story, I explained that the wound, just three weeks old and still a little red, was from removing a small tumor in my breast. No one questioned it further.

My wig was removed and my head wrapped in a towel as I lounged in a mineral bath. I was showered and wrapped in a blanket while a woman exfoliated my face with sandalwood powder and steamed me until I was glowing. Then I was led to a massage table and made to utterly relax under the hands of two experienced ladies. I believe they would have gone further than decorum allowed if I'd given the least sign I was interested.

After thoroughly having my head massaged as well, it was time for a manicure and pedicure. They put false nails on my fingers and painted them a shimmering pearl. I begged them not to make them too long or I wouldn't be able to eat. I believe the entire purpose of long fingernails is to disable women and make them dependent on their escort (male) for even the simplest tasks, like buttoning a button. Or unbuttoning it for that matter.

During my manicure, I was shown a selection of three dresses chosen for me by the shoppers. I also brought a new bikini and pareu. I tried on the gowns and was shocked at my appearance, nonetheless choosing a pale green dress that even went well with the new bikini. Not that I'd be wearing them at the same time.

Madam Wilson herself took care of my wig and makeup. When it was finished and I tried on the new dress and high-heeled sandals, I couldn't possibly recognize myself. Only Stevie had done such an expert job on my makeup. I have subtle disguises that are no more than a different wig, like I'd worn to the Condo in the beginning. Until Oksamma knocked it off my head and it went sailing over Seattle. I have a very good male disguise. I have my Riley Finn ID that simply modifies my appearance a little. And I have an older woman disguise and ID I've never used. She's Peg Chester. Look it up.

But one disguise I had never attempted was glamorous. What I saw in the mirror was definitely in the Bond girl category. I just hoped I didn't end up like most of them. It wasn't so radical that it would offend the sensibilities of an older and reserved Rentz, but... I sparkled. Part of that was the jeweled eyebrows Madam Wilson gave me. I don't have eyebrows and penciling them in was always risky. Putting jewels over the shadow of the brow, though was brilliant. She glued on fake eyelashes and did eyeshadow that gave my eyes that smoky look that when I try myself just looks like I got a black eye. Seeing I didn't have pierced ears, she glued on a matching set of jewels that ran down the slope of my ear to the lobe.

I tried on the dress and caught my breath. How do you wear this without blushing all the time? It's pretty much transparent silk and cut so tight I couldn't carry a credit card without making a bulge. The idea of a bra is out of the question and the panties aren't worth mentioning. So, in *Miss Congeniality*, where does Sandra Bullock keep pulling her wallet, gun, and handcuffs out of while she's wearing those costumes?

As a last touch, Madam pulled the front of my dress down, exposing my breasts. I'd been naked most of the day anyway, but I wasn't sure what was happening until she mashed a slightly pink pasty, exactly the size of my areola, onto my nipples. I breathed a sigh of relief. Without those, my nipples stuck out under the thin silk of the dress like two beacons on very small hills.

After being shown tricks for getting the dress on and off, which was a task in itself, I dressed in the bikini and sarong, thanked Madam Wilson and the ladies of the spa profusely, and went back to my room.

Searched

I WONDER IF the reason Jon wanted me in the spa all day was so he could have my room searched. It's not the mess that Cinnamon described the office as. It was the kind of careful job Jordan did when he searched the office and my apartment. I wouldn't have noticed but there were things that weren't quite right. Clothes put in the closet facing the wrong direction on the hanger. The mattress of the bed not quite square on the box springs. Whoever came in did a thorough job.

What did they find out?

The tells I left on my hiding place for my disguise and alternate ID were undisturbed, so it seems my basic cover is good. I made no secret about having my boyfriend with me, so the men's clothes in my closet are okay. Of course, no one has seen the boyfriend since I checked in. If they were expecting to find him in the room, they missed.

I used the tile surrounding the fan in the bathroom to put my disguises and passports in the ceiling. They looked in the ceiling in the closet. Dust had fallen down from it to the shelf. But the bathroom hiding place is not visible from that vantage. I know because I checked.

It makes me a little queasy about going to the party with Jon this evening but I can't find anything that would give me away. My regular makeup bag was rifled through but the only thing out of the ordinary in it is the spirit gum I usually use to keep my wig firmly in place. With the adhesive Madam used, I could dive in the pool with this on and it would stay put.

Well, there's nothing for it but to walk boldly into the den of vipers. I've got my bikini on with a lacy pareu wrapped around my waist. My dress and purse are in a hanging bag and it's time to go meet Jon when he pulls up in his luxury golf cart. Pretty much all transportation on the island is by golf cart or bicycle.

Wish me luck!

{21}
Facing the bitch

WHY AM I SO MUCH BETTER at getting myself into trouble than getting out of it? Where did that bug come from? How am I supposed to run in high heels? And what is *she* doing here?

———————|—+–+–+–+++++++–+–+–+——

A matter of opinion

IT ALL STARTED at the Muffin-top's villa.

Jon picked me up in a six-seater golf cart complete with a driver and two guys who rode on the back with sunglasses and Aloha shirts. They are either his staff or guards. Maybe both. When we got to the villa, we had to pass through security like the one installed at the Condo. Jon had already warned me not to bother bringing my cellphone. All I had with me was my Riley Finn driver's license and some lipstick Madam had given me to freshen my look. They were in a tiny clutch along with the underwear I'd need beneath my dress this evening.

I tell you, this lady's got balls. Every man who showed up, young or old, had at least one girl in her twenties on his arm. Besides the 'dates,' there were a dozen hired eye candy girls by the pool. Young, beautiful, and even more exposed than the dates in our tiny bikinis. Maybe the idea of topless sunbathing was supposed to inspire the rest of us but none of the other dates bit and neither did I. But there, as proud as if she'd just won the Miss

America pageant, was Miss Muffin-top in a bikini that was a size and a half too small for her. And the men all drooled over her while a dozen topless hookers sat by the water being neglected.

The villa was island chic with a lot of terracotta and bamboo on the floors. Air-cooling misters sprayed over the rooms and poolside while huge overhead fans moved the air around so we didn't stifle. One of the topless beauties met us as soon as we entered and offered to show me around. Apparently, she was a hostess. Jon released my arm and said he'd wait at the bar. Savon, the hostess, showed me where the bedrooms were, the restrooms, the dining room, and finally the huge indoor pool. I noted there were a bunch of huge guys who didn't look the least bit native in their loincloths and big leaf fans. They probably helped cool the air around the beauties they fanned, but from the way their eyes kept shifting around, I could tell they were guards and were probably listening as intently to what was going on around them and the chatterboxes who lounged there.

And that was my first big surprise of the evening. Across the pool was a small group of women I recognized. Delta was there with two others from the Condo whose names I couldn't remember. But the real shock was seeing my best friend, Teri, chatting with them.

I excused myself from Savon quickly and went into the nearest restroom. I looked at myself in the mirror critically. Teri's seen me dressed in a lot of different outfits when we go out to play but I didn't think she'd seen me looking anywhere near the way I did now. I was close to six feet tall in the heels I wore. My bikini top didn't have a lot to conceal but it didn't conceal much either. I was thankful it covered the pasties. The bottom was a thong that cut between my ass cheeks in as uncomfortable a position as I could imagine but I had a sarong tied around my waist that just bared my left leg from the sandals to my waist. I'd assumed I'd have to wear a Hijab or even a Niqab to keep her from recognizing me when I tried to collect on my bet. This was about the opposite and showed me in all my glory. I wasn't sure a red wig and gaudy makeup was going to keep her from just yelling out my name.

"Well, let's go, girl," I said to my reflection in my haughtiest Bostonian accent. "Jon's waiting." I held my head high and took to heart my own advice on disguise. *Rock it like you own it.* I did.

I joined my date at the bar where he was chatting with Stan Metzger of the big publishing conglomerate in Seattle. I'd read in Forbes about him being head of eleven newspapers and a magazine publishing company in Des Moines. He hadn't made the Forbes 100 cutoff but he was well within the top 500 wealthiest men in the world.

"Let's ask Miss Finn," Jon said when I stroked his arm in greeting. "Miss Finn, meet Mr. Metz." *Hmm. None of these guys had any imagination when it came to their aliases.* I smiled at the man and took his hand. "As far as your generation is concerned, what is the most reliable and opinion-shaping source of news available to you?"

"Oh. Mr. Rentz, Mr. Metz, I don't think my opinion on that matter is typical of my generation," I said, trying to collect my thoughts.

"Please tell us and describe the difference," Metz said.

"Well, we have a reputation of shaping most of our opinions based on Facebook memes and Twitter posts. I'm afraid that is not an entirely unfair characterization," I said. "I believe, however, it is more a way of solidifying opinion than creating it. People decide what they want to believe and then search out sources, friends, and communities who agree with them. Within that community, memes and posts are passed around that keep building up the veracity of the opinion, regardless of its validity."

"Well-spoken young woman," Metz said—not to me but to Jon. "She could go far. May I continue?" Jon nodded to him. "Miss Finn, what is the difference in your opinion from that of your generation?"

"I am not always successful, Mr. Metz, but I try not to have opinions. I have a great many questions but prefer to base my actions on actual research that reveals facts without tainting it with preconceived notions. I've seen too often how things become ingrained in a person's mind to such an extent that they cannot tolerate any fact that disagrees with them. I'm only interested in verifiable data."

"Perhaps we should talk later about your interest in fact-gathering. As a news organization, my company is always on the lookout for someone who has both the skill and passion to get to the truth," Metz said.

"That isn't appropriate for our social gathering," Jon said. "We should set a time up tomorrow. I just wanted to introduce the two of you. Miss Finn is an extraordinary woman—if you will go so far as to trust my 'opinion'." We all had a chuckle and I faded back behind Jon as the men continued to drink and chat. I think I'd just been recruited.

Eavesdropping

SAVON COLLECTED ME at dusk and suggested we join a group for a walk along the shore as the stars came out. Half a dozen of us carried our sandals as we walked to the water's edge, trying to ignore the three men in loincloths who followed not far behind. They ranged themselves out more to create a barrier between us and anything else. I wondered what the hell they thought we'd do out here or who we'd meet.

In this little group, there seemed to be no differences between the two bare-breasted hostesses and the four dates in our skimpy swimwear. The chatter was easy and I thought how easy it would be to assume these girls were just like me—just trying to do her job and solve some great mystery. For as smart as they seemed, none of them seemed to have the least concept that the men in this meeting had no business meeting together on an isolated island with a woman who ruled it like a queen bee.

We watched the brilliant display of stars light up the eastern sky and then heard a conch being blown by the pool.

"It's time to get you ladies ready for dinner," Savon said. We walked back to the villa with our bodyguards keeping watch. At the pool, I excused myself.

"I need the restroom," I said. "Having all that water lapping around me did something to my bladder." The girls laughed and Savon told me which bedroom was my changing room. I soon discovered a weakness in island construction. The bathroom was barely proof against being seen on the toilet. Soundproof, it definitely was not. I heard voices outside and realized the back of the bathroom room I'd ducked into masked a private patio where the Muffin-top was holding conversations with three of the men on the Committee.

"I thought we took care of him," one said. "You told us it was taken care of."

"Apparently, he didn't go down as easily as I thought," Brenda said. "He's still loose somewhere and I don't like it a bit." It took no instruction to understand they were upset that I'd gotten away at the Condo. I was fortunate none of them knew James Whitcomb was one of my aliases. Even if they caught me, they would still think he was on the loose.

"Where is he?"

"He's slippery. Didn't leave any tracks. But I have a clue. Angel left Seattle a few days ago. If anyone knows, she does."

"So, where is she?"

"Hmm. My husband bought her a property in Croatia. I don't know the exact location but I'm betting that's where Angel escaped to. She should help us… if she knows what's good for her."

I scampered out of the toilet and headed to my assigned dressing room. Why did they connect Angel with me? Of course. She was the first person I'd visited when I put on the James Whitcomb disguise. I'll bet they had some kind of access to Angel's security camera or Davy identified me. *Damn!* They didn't use my name, so maybe they still didn't know me.

When I reached the bedrooms, Savon pointed me to the right one.

"I've laid your dress out for you, Miss Finn. If there is anything you need help with, please let me know. I'll be right outside." It seemed almost as if our hostesses were also part of our assigned bodyguards. They certainly hovered near us when we were not with our dates.

Of course, it turned out that Teri was one of the girls assigned the same bedroom to dress in. I'm sure we made quite a sight, all trying to get dressed in the same little space. Fortunately, there wasn't much for any of us to put on. I slipped on my little thong and brazenly stripped off my top and sarong. It only took a second to slide the slinky dress over my head and shake it down my body. A couple girls with bigger boobs were having a little struggle.

From the laughter and voices, I'd say most of the girls thought this was the most natural thing in the world but I saw Teri was spending a lot of time trying to cover up more of her body than the dress did. I decided it was time to move in and face the music. It must have been the distraction of the dress that did it. I can't imagine how else Teri could have missed recognizing me when I spoke, even though I carefully kept my voice modulated in that Boston accent.

"Don't worry," I said to her, taking the scarf from her hand and tying it around her waist instead of her shoulders. It looked very fetching. "You'll look out of place if you try to cover up too much. Just look at the others."

"I'm so nervous," Teri responded. "I met this guy at a game the other night and I don't know why, but I agreed to go on his yacht with him. I thought it was in Puget Sound but it turned out we drove to Boeing Field and took off in a private jet to New Orleans. We boarded the yacht and sailed down here. I would have freaked out if there hadn't been half a dozen of us. I'm just so new at this."

"Playing with rich guys is a different experience. They are so into their toys."

"Here," she said, "let me help you with your corsage. There's one for each of us."

There'd been an orchid laid out with each of our dresses and Teri pinned mine on. I returned the favor. She tugged it down the strap a bit so it slightly concealed her left nipple beneath the fabric of the dress. It seemed to make her feel better.

"Well, let's go meet the predators," I said. Teri still hadn't shown a glimmer of recognition and I wasn't sure she'd actually looked at me yet.

Gotta run

THERE WAS ANOTHER security screening before we walked into the dining room. A guy passed a wand over each of us, paying special attention to asses and cleavage. Maybe that was for security. For Pete's sake, where were we going to conceal anything.

Imagine my surprise when the damn thing beeped when he passed it over my left breast. He came back and passed it over again, checking the wand. Next thing I knew, I was being led out into the next room. The guy was polite but he let the back of his hand linger a little too long on my breast as he unpinned my corsage. Jon and Brenda came into the room where my flower was being dissected.

"What's the problem?" Jon asked.

"We're reading an electronic device on her," the guard answered.

"Where would she conceal an electronic device?" Brenda asked. "She's barely covered."

"It's here," the guard answered. He tapped the flower's little water holder on the table and a tiny metal device fell out of it.

"What's going on?" The newcomer was Geoff Gilliam, the sports play-boy from the yacht. Apparently, Teri's date. Well, I understood that a little now. He bought the team with inherited money, is half the age of any of the other men here, and is pretty sexy looking.

"We've got a listening device on this pretty little thing," Brenda said. "Who were you planning to broadcast to, Honey?"

"I didn't know anything about this," I said. "I just put the flower on in the bedroom." I was truly horrified. It had to have been planted and distributed with the flowers. But was it random or did someone plan for me to be investigated? Guilty conscience. Brenda, at least, was showing no sign of recognition. When we'd last met, I was a blonde in a business suit and was dismissed as Dag's bimbo.

"Sure you don't," Geoff said. I could see a mean streak about him and was worried about Teri. Sometimes she can really pick them. "Who are you really and why do you have a listening device in your flower?"

"Come, come, now Geoff," Jon said. "The flowers were delivered hours ago. I'll bet the device came in with them."

"Yes. That must be what happened," I said, a little too anxiously.

"You're hiding something," Geoff said. "I can always tell when a woman is lying to me."

"What do you suggest, Geoff?" Brenda asked, sidling up to him and slipping her hand through his arm. "She may already know too much. Who knows how long she's been listening in with that thing?"

"No, really," I said.

"Shut up, bitch," Geoff said.

"Really, Geoff," Jon began.

"You're too soft, old man," Geoff said. "You know how important security is. That's why we're meeting way the hell out here instead of in Seattle. Load her up and take her out to the *Helen of Troy*. I'll drop her off on an island sometime tomorrow and we'll see how well she gets her information back. I'll bet she's a reporter."

"What would a reporter be doing out here?" Jon asked.

"Think, Jon," Brenda said. "What reporter wouldn't want to be in this company? I'll bet she has a story already. I agree with Geoff. You don't even have to wait for an island to drop her off as far as I'm concerned. Drop her in the middle of the ocean."

There comes a time when you should run and I'd reached that moment. I gave dear concerned Jon a shove into the security guard and blasted past, headed out through the kitchen. Running in an evening gown and high heels is not to be recommended. I hit the pool deck and skidded, falling off the heels and nearly twisting my ankle. As I bent to release the strap from my ankle, I was hit from the side by Savon. *That bitch!* I was too far off balance to right myself and fell into the pool. She crooked her finger at me to beckon me to the edge of the pool where one of the guys snapped cuffs on me and lifted me out of the water.

The dress had done little for my modesty in the first place. Soaking wet, it did considerably less.

{22}
On the run... again

S O MUCH FOR SOLIDARITY AMONG WOMEN. Girls looking out for each other. The bitch just stood there gloating at me after pushing me in the pool. What kind of a name is Savon anyway? Sounds like a grocery store coupon. She's just a goon with tits.

———————————

Escape

TWO MEN PROPELLED me out on the pier and into a small motor boat, which they launched toward the *Helen of Troy*. My gut was telling me this captor was even worse than Bradley. Geoff Gilliam was not only a playboy, he was a sadist. *God! How did Teri get mixed up with him?*

By the time I was ushered into a cabin, I'd had hands all over my body in very ungentlemanly ways. They unfastened the cuffs in the cabin but locked the door behind me. All the while there'd been a running commentary about what they would do to me, 'when the boss was through.' Apparently, Geoff had rules about not soiling the merchandise before he got his filthy hands on it. A few moments later, the door opened and a towel was thrown through it. Then it was closed and locked again.

I stripped out of the wet dress and dried with the towel, checking the critical parts of my makeup—eyebrows, eyelashes, and wig. I could do without the jewels, but they seemed pretty stable. I needed clothes now that I was out of the wet dress. Various swimwear for both men and women hung in the closet and I chose a one-piece to cover myself with. I wrapped a terrycloth robe around me and started looking for a way out.

It was an inside cabin with no porthole making the only exit the door I came in through. I rummaged all through the closet and found nothing more than a hanger I could use as a weapon. I paced back and forth for nearly an hour before I heard the rattle of the door being opened again. I prepared myself this time to take out whoever came through the door. The door opened and I grabbed the woman who entered and threw her on the bed locking her arms behind her and looking toward the still-open door.

"Friend! Friend!" she cried. "I came to help."

"Teri?" I let her up and she turned to look at me.

"It really is you!" she exclaimed. "When I saw you run toward the pool, I suddenly thought 'She's just like Deb.' Then I figured it had to be."

"Thanks for not blowing my cover," I said. "But this is dangerous for you. I've got to get out of here."

"There's no place to go," Teri said. "There's only one sentry on board as far as I can tell. He's up on the bridge. All the rest of the crew and the girls are at the party. They have all the boats with them."

"How did you get out here?" I asked.

"I was trying to figure out a way all through the first course. I finally poured salt in my water and drank it in a single swallow. Then threw up. I complained it was the shellfish. Geoff swore at me and said it was the alcohol and I was dismissed from the party. There were plenty of other girls who would like to have my place. He told one of his security people to take me to the boat to sleep it off." Teri paused to breathe.

"But how did you unlock my door?" I asked.

"I picked the guard's pocket as he was feeling me up, supposedly helping me climb the ladder to the deck."

"I may have to find a place for you at DH Investigations," I laughed.

"No thanks. I regretted making this trip from the moment we reached Boeing Field. But there were six girls he was taking and I thought safety in numbers, you know? I tried to call you but all I got was voice mail."

"I haven't been checking lately. I have so much to fill you in on. But now we need to leave. You should come with me. It's not safe for you here." Teri quickly changed into a swimsuit and robe then stopped by another stateroom to grab her purse. We made our way onto deck, staying in the shadows. I couldn't see the sentry on guard and that made me nervous.

"Okay, tell me what to do," Teri said.

"Since there's no boat, we'll have to swim to shore," I said. "Come on. It's not that far."

"I can't swim."

"Teri! You rollerblade, play soccer, play hockey, and run but you can't swim? You're kidding!"

"None of those take place in water. I've always been afraid of the water," she answered. "That made sailing down here hell."

"We'll take a flotation device then. I'll pull you to shore."

"Why don't you take my boat, instead," a voice spoke from the shadows. Teri screamed and I went into a defensive crouch as Ray Hawkins stepped out of the shadow. "I came to rescue you but it seems I'm a little late."

"Why would you want to rescue me?" I asked warily.

"Well, I got you into this mess," he answered. "Least I could do was get you out."

"It wasn't your suggestion that made me decide to go," I said, not willing to flatter him with having a good idea.

"No, but it was me that planted the transmitter in the flowers. I had to wait until I'd recorded enough of the dinner conversation to make it worth my time to come out here." He motioned to the ladder on the offshore side of the boat where a little dinghy bobbed alongside.

"Can we all fit in that?" Teri asked.

"We'll have to," Ray insisted. We dropped quietly down into the boat and he rowed us south before turning toward shore near San Pedro. "You two should get out of here," he said. "I need to mop some things up here before I go."

"I need to go back to my room and pack. Teri, you can wear some of my clothes. Do you have your passport?"

"Yes, in my bag. Never travel without your passport, my mother always said."

"Your mother never said that," I laughed.

"All right, I made it up."

"Ladies, please," Ray interrupted. "Let's get Miss Finn packed and get out of here. I'll arrange a boat to the mainland."

Teri and I ran to my room and started throwing things into my bag. I tossed her a pair of beach pants and pulled on my khaki shorts over the swimsuit.

"I'm sorry I don't have more clothes for you. You can pick some up at the airport."

"Deb, most of these clothes are men's clothes. What's going on?"

"Let's just say that you were the last one on my list I had to fool with a disguise. And it worked until I got shoved into the pool." I crawled up on the toilet and removed the panel in the ceiling where I pulled down my makeup kits, padding, and extra passports.

Teri just shook her head in disbelief. Ray knocked and I fastened the suitcase closed.

"I have a few contacts down here and a friend who will take us across the channel. I'm going with you as far as the airport. Friend or not, I don't trust what would happen to two young women traveling in the dark."

"I don't want to leave from Belize," I said without thinking. "Teri can fly home from Belize City but I don't want to be tracked from here."

"And what do you suggest?" Ray asked sarcastically. "Sprouting your own wings?"

"I'll get a car and drive up to Mexico. I'll leave from there."

"Oh, just great," he responded. I had the feeling he was regretting helping us.

We argued about it most of the way from Ambergris Caye to Belize City. We argued about it some more on the way to the airport. Teri was scared but I assured her she would be fine and to look up Cinnamon when she got to my office. But I was determined to rent a car and head north.

I got Teri out into the boarding area for a plane to Houston a few hours away from takeoff and headed out to rent a car. Ray informed me there weren't any.

"What do you mean? I can't rent a car in Belize?"

"No."

"Why not?"

"Because I rented the last one."

"You?"

"I can't let you drive alone through Belize and the Yucatan. I told you I don't trust what would happen to a woman traveling alone down here.

Together, we're another couple touring the Mayan ruins. Alone, you'd just be prey."

We argued about that most of the way from Belize City to the Mexican border. Now I'm sleepy and have no idea how I'm going to get from Mexico to Croatia. I've got to warn Angel that Brenda knows where she is.

Ray dropped me at the Holiday Inn in Chetumal about 3:00 a.m. and then took off like a bat out of hell. Apparently, he wanted to be back on the island before people stirred this morning. I slept till about eight and then made travel arrangements to fly from here to Mexico City and from there to Croatia.

———+ +++++++++++ +———

Now you see me...

I NEEDED TO clean up my act and become Deb Riley before I made another move. I was glad Ray had gone back to San Pedro without having penetrated my disguise. I'd had to warn Teri not to call me Deb and she seemed to get along okay with Riley.

It suddenly soaked into me that I'd been taking incredible risks. I fled to the airport in Seattle disguised as James Whitcomb. Making it through security and customs was nothing short of a miracle. *Fool's luck.* I changed identities on Ambergris Caye and ended up fleeing for my life as Riley Finn with a strange, if not unattractive man. I entered Mexico under false identity. But now I'm headed for Croatia. I'll connect in Mexico City and in Paris on my way to Zagreb. I'm not going to risk getting snagged by some European police department in disguise. It's time to become Deb Riley and hope no one checks for a Mexican visa in that name. I stripped off all the jewels still plastered to my face and my red wig. The shower was awesome.

The clothes in my suitcases are totally inappropriate for the chilly weather of Croatia. According to the web, temperatures have been in the thirties and forties through most of that region. So much for the balmy seventies and eighties of Belize. I thought the Dalmatian coast was supposed to be a sunny Mediterranean port!

I went shopping for warm girl-clothes. It's hard to find regular clothes in a Mexican resort town. Looking at myself in a mirror, I saw the face of a blonde I hardly recognized. I hadn't seen her in two weeks! I bought a *huipil*, a kind of shapeless native poncho blouse, and a print skirt. I also picked up slacks, some underwear, and a wool serape. I don't want to get caught in the cold with nothing to keep me warm. I pulled a *rebozo* scarf that covered my head and shoulders and ended up looking like another crazy *Yanqui* girl who had to dress native in order to go home. I went to the airport and checked my luggage through all the way to Croatia.

I suppose being dressed in these exotic clothes made me think more about my disguise. I was Deb Riley and didn't think anyone was tracking me, but I don't know Ray that well. He saved our bacon in San Pedro but sometimes he looked at me in a way that made me very uncomfortable. I watched the Mexican women who were boarding planes. There weren't that many who were traveling by air. It was mostly men. As a result, they acted… small. That's the only way I can describe it. They drew in on themselves. I, in my typical stand-tall American body, stuck out among them in spite of being dressed similarly. I started thinking differently. I drew inward and shrank. Head bowed. Hands grasping a carry-on bag I'd just purchased in front of me. Careful not to look furtive. Just blend in with the other women. Look small. Don't make eye contact.

Gotta board the plane.

{23}
Flight Time

T HAT BASTARD'S FOLLOWING ME. That's the only possible explanation. So, who does he work for really? He wasn't meeting with the Committee but Jon recognized him as a wanna-be. Is Jordan having me tailed? He could give a girl a heads up.

———— ·|· ·|· ·|·|·|·||||||·|·|· ·|· ·|· ————

Headed east

WHEN I GOT off the plane in Mexico City, looking small as my five-nine can go, the first person I spotted was Ray Hawkins. He was standing behind a pillar in the airport scanning the people getting off the plane. I fell in step with a nice Mexican man and pretended to be talking to him, keeping him between Ray and me.

When I was shopping for flights, I looked for other local airports. Merida was the nearest and it looked like a three-hour drive from Chetumal. Or maybe there was another flight from Chetumal. Whatever, he was in the Mexico City airport watching for me.

Okay, so with luck he was watching for the redhead Riley Finn he met in San Pedro. I don't think he recognized me but who is he, anyway?

I'm flying first class to Croatia, cost be damned. I sat in the first class passenger lounge watching out the window for any sign he was near. I didn't see him anywhere but I'll feel a lot better when I get on the plane to Paris.

I bought a SIM at Duty Free and called Cinnamon who was more than happy to hear from me.

"Sugar, where are you?" she exclaimed when I got through.

"Mexico City," I answered. "What's up?"

"When do I get to go jet-setting like you?" she asked. "Or with you?"

"I'm sure you'll get a chance," I said. "Anything new happening?"

"The office is about cleaned up. Do you want me to keep any of the furniture? I've put everything small enough to fit in a box aside for you to look at but there is the torn-up sofa, chairs, and desk."

"This might sound crazy but I'd like you to hire someone to put them in storage for me. I want to be sure nothing is hidden in anything."

"Whatever you say, boss. When are you coming home? I miss you."

"It will be a few days yet. I'm going to visit Angel."

"That lucky bitch!"

"Cinnamon! I've put her in danger and I need to go warn her," I said.

"Well, Angel always got whatever she wanted," Cinnamon pouted. "You'd get the same reaction from any of the girls."

"Honey," I said soothingly, "when you were cleaning up the mess, did you find the TV remote by any chance?" I'd had the uncomfortable idea gnawing at the back of my mind for several days that if they'd taken the remote, I didn't know how to get into the vault. I'd been able to reset the servers remotely but I didn't want imagine trying to get into it without that little device.

"Funny. Yeah. Couldn't believe they took the TV without it. I don't think men know how to operate a TV if it doesn't have a remote."

"Just goes to show you. It could be a clue, so make sure it's in the box."

"Will do. By the way, that nice Jordan Grant came by."

"Did he now? And what did Mr. Grant want." I'm sure the satellite carrying our call frosted over.

"I think he wants to ask me out on a date," Cinnamon said. "He's handsome."

"He's way too old for you, Cinnamon!" I said a little too vehemently. What was I thinking?

"Jealous?" she teased.

"No! I'm not interested in Mr. Grant. And I won't date a client. Now why did he come around?"

"He said he was worried about you. Frankly, I'd say you should be worried about him."

"Why?"

"He was on crutches."

"What happened?" I was alarmed. Jordan always seemed so indestructible. I still remembered him shooting Oksamma when a second later, Oksamma would have shot me or Dag or both.

"Apparently, he was rushing somewhere early Friday morning over on the Eastside where all the power was out. He went through an intersection where there was no light and someone plowed into him from the side. He's got a broken leg but said he was all right otherwise. He said if he hadn't broken his leg, he'd have gone to Belize after you himself."

"Wait a minute. How did he know I was in Belize? Cinnamon?"

"Don't ask me. I never said a word. I didn't confirm your whereabouts either. I just said when you called in, you didn't say where you were. I played dumb blonde. I think he liked it."

"Oh, come on," I said. "Jordan likes strong women with intelligence."

"Like you, you mean," Cinnamon said. "Don't worry, Sugar. I learned my lessons in the Condo well. I'm smart enough to know when to be clever. That's enough. Besides, I didn't do anything. But if he asks me out, I might just say yes."

"All right. Here's an opportunity for you to talk to him again. Sometime after six-thirty tonight call him. In fact, make it after seven. Tell him you heard from me and I'm on my way to Croatia to visit Angel. She's in danger from the bad guys—or the bad girl. Most of the guys are old and slow and squeamish. All except the one who would have drowned me in the high seas. I'll let him know when I get there." I wanted Jordan as backup but I didn't want to be followed without knowing who's there.

"You got it. Anything else?"

"Yes. Call Teri and make sure she got home safely, please. She can tell you all about our big adventure in Belize."

"She got to go with you? Deb-bie…" Cinnamon broke off quickly. "Oops. Sorry Sugar. You can spank me for that when you get home." I swear she giggled.

Time to board.

Zagreb

AT TEN P.M. I was wide awake in a Zagreb hotel. There was nothing about it that made it different from any other hotel I'd ever seen. Except the ten-hour time change made my poor body think it was noon and time to get to work.

I called to check in with Cinnamon. She was glad to hear from me and her temperament was less volatile, though no less flirty.

"Hey, Sugar! It's nice you called little old me again," she said when she answered the phone.

"Hey yourself, Cinnamon. It's good to hear the voice of home a little more often," I answered. I did like talking to her.

"Aw. I'm home," she sighed. "I like that. So, come home."

"As soon as I can get this settled. I just don't want to think Angel could be in danger because of me. Stupid disguises."

"Did *she* kiss you, too?"

"No," I chuckled. "I told her I was gay."

"Would you make up your mind, girl? Straight girl, gay guy, straight girl in drag pretending to be a gay guy. Just finish and come home."

"I'll do that. Did you call Jordan?"

"Yes. He swore in my presence! Right there on the phone. I thought he had better breeding than that. You really made him mad."

"At least he knows approximately where I am. I'll text him with an exact location when I find it," I said. Now that I was back in my own body, so to speak, I wasn't nearly as cautious about letting Jordan know where I was.

"He said he's sending someone after you as backup."

"Who?"

"He just said you'd recognize him when you see him."

"Great. Now who could that be?"

"I don't know but he said he had to make calls and hung up on me. Should I call him back?"

"Don't sound so hopeful," I answered. "I'll text him."

"Did you really fall in a pool when you tried to escape the party?"

"I was pushed into the pool. By that Amazon warrior Brenda had watching over me. The bitch."

"That dress! Teri told me it must have cost a fortune."

"Too bad. The dress was the least of my worries. I left it on the boat where they took me." I hesitated before I went on. "Look, Cinnamon. You know a lot of these guys, er… professionally. What do you think of Geoff Gilliam?"

"Mr. All-Talk-And-No-Action?"

"What do you mean by that?"

"All the girls know he talks macho and is ultra-rude talking about sex but when it comes down to it, not one girl reports having been touched by him. The girls figure he's a closeted gay guy so we do our best to keep his reputation up. It's a good thing he didn't meet you in your Mr. J disguise. He'd have liked that." She laughed and I had to join in. But that news just didn't jive with what I'd experienced. I felt certain I'd have been dumped at sea if I hadn't escaped.

"Did Teri say anything about him? Is he into hurting people?"

"Like I said, all talk and no action. Nobody has ever been hurt by him that we know. Of course, all the girls have their own limits and we don't go around talking about the guys. It's part of the code. But if any of them forced a girl to something she didn't want, we'd all shut him down."

"Okay. I'll take you at your word but the guy really scares me."

"So, where are you now? What can I do to help?"

"This is really dumb but I just remembered it. Did you find my car keys in the office?"

"Car keys? Other than the ones you gave me? There was a set on the floor in the front office come to think of it."

"Good. I couldn't remember where I dropped them. My car is in the Pike Place Garage. Could you go over and bail it out? I've got a parking spot at my apartment." I gave her the directions and told her I'd wire money to her account if she'd give me the details. She just laughed.

"Sugar, I'll turn in my expense report when you get home. Anybody who drives a '94 Dodge probably has less money than I do. I'm not hurting as long as you come back." I didn't do anything to dissuade her of her opinion. I'd discovered Dag made sure I had enough to do my job.

"Oh, one more thing," Cinnamon said. "Mr. Andersen came by this morning. He said he had the final papers for you to sign and something about expecting your thesis by the first. Ring a bell?" My thesis. *Damn!* I couldn't remember doing any work on it at all since Dag died. Somehow it just hadn't seemed important. Of course, the readers would want it at least a week before my jury the second week of January. I needed to wrap up this little adventure I was on and get home and to work. Life had to go on whether I was a detective or not. The other reasons Lars might have had to come to the office were things I didn't want to think about.

"So, did you want to date Lars, too?" I asked. "I'm pretty sure he's single."

"We all have standards, Sugar," she answered. "I'll leave Lars to you while I handle Jordan."

"You're an evil woman," I said. She agreed and hung up.

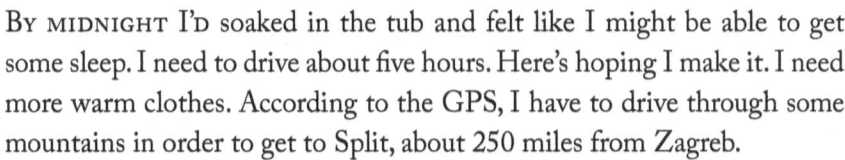

By MIDNIGHT I'D soaked in the tub and felt like I might be able to get some sleep. I need to drive about five hours. Here's hoping I make it. I need more warm clothes. According to the GPS, I have to drive through some mountains in order to get to Split, about 250 miles from Zagreb.

'Night!

{24}
Guardian Angel

JETLAG HIT ME big time and I had three cups of coffee thick enough to cut with a knife before I got in my rental car and headed southeast. I got a fast car and drove too fast all the way from Zagreb to Split on the A1. The mountain pass wasn't as bad as I expected but spooky as hell. A five-mile tunnel. Before I took off, I sent a quick text to Jordan to let him know where I was headed. I want him to know, but I don't want him to get there before I do.

The big lie

IT TOOK OVER five hours to get to Split. Then I decided to enhance my wardrobe a little before continuing to Island Brac where Angel's villa is. I doubt she knows I have the information on her location. It was part of the details Dag left in his accounting files from when he transferred money for Simon. This place was nowhere near where the money was transferred but Dag didn't let that stop him from locating it in Simon's files. The guy was almost as devious as me. Damn him for dying!

But if Dag located it, it shouldn't surprise me that Brenda knew about it and could track down Angel as well. Nothing is safe from prying eyes.

It's as cold here as in Seattle, though I don't think it's going to snow for Christmas. I'd like to be home by then.

With new clothes and a full belly, I caught the 45-minute ferry to Island Brac.

—————++++++++HHHHH++++++—————

It was a short trip from the terminal to the villa. When I saw it, I thought I'd reached a dead end. The villa is near the center of an immense stone structure with an iron gate separating it from the street not far from the marina. I wasn't sure how I'd get in until I walked up, pushed the gate and listened to it creak open. It wasn't locked. That needed to change.

I walked up the stone steps to a massive front door and knocked.

Angel opened the door after a few moments and I don't know which of us was more surprised to see the other. I assumed there would be servants; she assumed I was anybody else other than me. We stared for several heartbeats the both broke out in a grin.

"Deb! How did you…? Why…? I don't know what to say!" Angel said.

"You could start by inviting me in. It's cold out here."

"Come in! God, it's good to see you! It's only been, what, two weeks and already I miss everyone."

We went into the house and I started to see what an immense place it was inside. It was an older structure but had been completely modernized inside. The furnishings were impeccable, of course. I wondered how much of it had been prepared in advance and how much Angel had done in the two weeks since I last saw her. I couldn't tell but I had a feeling the place had been prepared a long time ago.

She offered me a club soda and we sat in the living room to chat.

"So, what have you been up to since we last spoke? I was so panicked back then, I wasn't thinking straight. You should have come in disguise. You'd have been able to fool me completely, showing up here. I'd have never guessed it was you."

"You didn't," I said. "But collecting on the bet isn't what brings me here. Brenda and the Committee know you're here and I think they suspect you may be sheltering a guy who is a threat to them." Angel blanched. "I couldn't call you, so I came to warn you. They're sending someone in to clean up loose ends."

I expected Angel to ask who they thought she was sheltering. I intended to expose how I'd fooled her as James Whitcomb and at least we'd have a good laugh about that. But instead she jumped up from her seat and headed for the door. Before she got there, it swung open and a man walked through.

"I heard," he said, catching Angel in his arms. "And who is this lovely creature?" He stepped out around Angel to look at me and I caught my breath. I'd only seen photos of him but even though he now wore a full beard and his hair was dyed coal black, I recognized him from the pictures in Brenda's bedroom I was looking at the very-much-alive ghost of Simon Barnett.

"You!" I gasped. "It's you they're after, not me! You are supposed to be dead!"

"Isn't it wonderful, Deb? I didn't know until I arrived here and he was waiting for me," Angel said. "I was as surprised as you. Only, I think I was pretty furious first."

"Not half as furious as I am," I exclaimed. "You let Dag die thinking he'd killed you. How could you do that? How could you use him and destroy him, you bastard? I'll kill you myself!" I was a little out of control. I looked for something I could attack him with but came up empty. I just stood there shaking.

Angel crossed the room and wrapped her arms around me and pulled me down to the sofa. I was so angry I was shaking and tears were streaming down my cheeks. I couldn't believe what I was seeing. Angel held me and I completely went to pieces. It was several minutes before I finally came down and saw Simon sitting in a chair opposite me, calmly sipping his drink.

"How could you?" I asked weakly. "Once a betrayer, always a betrayer."

"I didn't mean to," Simon said quietly. He actually hung his head. "Either time. You must be the assistant he was so enamored with. Angel told me about you. It's Deb, right?" I nodded. "Please believe me when I say I didn't expect Dag to die. He was the only person other than Angel I trusted. I thought sure he'd break the code on the thumb drive and then when he busted the Committee, I'd contact him and come out of hiding. I didn't realize he was that sick. I thought we had time."

"He died thinking he'd pulled the trigger that killed you. Brenda told him the code on the GPS set off the bomb in your plane."

"He did do that," Simon said. "I found the bomb before I took off. That oaf Oksamma didn't have much subtlety. I knew that plane like the back of my hand. I inspected it completely every time I flew. It was wired to blow up when someone accessed the GPS. I could have blown myself up if I'd switched it on once I was airborne. Once I realized Brenda was that serious about getting rid of me, I reset the trigger and flew in low over Cuba. I bailed out and let the plane explode. I'm still hurting from the twisted ankle but I have friends in Cuba who took care of me. When I heard Dag was dead, I gave up and headed for the villa here. I figured sooner or later Angel would show up. Then here she was, telling me the Committee was trying to track down whatever evidence I'd left behind and she ran."

"Well, get ready to run some more," I said. "Brenda held a meeting of the Committee in Belize and said she was sending someone dependable out to finish the job. I thought she was talking about finishing me and I came to warn Angel."

"Why would anyone want to finish you?" Simon asked. I looked at him for a long time.

"For one thing, I'm the one who broke the encryption code on your thumb drive." I thought I'd seen everything but Simon blew half his drink out his nose and dropped the glass on the stone floor where it shattered.

"I'll be go-to-hell!" he exclaimed, jumping up and wiping himself off. Angel scurried to the kitchen to get a broom and towels. So domestic. "You mean you tracked down all four tattoos? You figured out the sequence and secondary encryption? I figured Dag was the only one in the world who could break that! You did it?"

"Apparently I'm not as dumb a blonde as I look," I snarled.

"You are smarter than Dag looked," he said, "and that fucker was the only certified genius I ever met."

At the mention of Dag's name, I felt tears leaking out of my eyes again.

"Oh, JFC! Don't go crying again. I'm sorry about Dag. I really am. And I'm damned impressed with you. I wish we'd gotten you on the inside sooner. You could have run the whole operation at the Condo," Simon said. Some compliment. I didn't even acknowledge it.

"Well, I guess you don't need me now," I said standing. "Message delivered. You're on your own. Brenda's sending someone to make sure you're really dead this time. Good luck. I can't believe I thought she was after me." I turned and headed toward the door.

"Deb, wait!" Angel said. "Honey, don't leave. Please stay with us tonight. If you still feel you have to go in the morning, I'll help make arrangements. You know, I'm a travel agent." She grinned at me and held out her arms.

—+—+-+-+-+HIIH+-+-+—+—

MAYBE IT'S JUST because I'm so tired, jetlagged, stoked on caffeine, and emotionally strung out. I let her convince me. I'm in one of the villa's eight bedrooms, having had a big meal and a glass of wine. I'll sort the rest out tomorrow.

{25}
Wash it all away

I DIDN'T WANT TO GET OUT OF BED. It was a comfortable bed and I felt like I hadn't slept well in a month. I woke up during the night, cried some more, and went back to sleep. Dag died believing he killed Simon but Simon was just hiding out. I'm trying to be rational about it and it just isn't working. I don't trust him.

———————————————

Coffee

I DON'T KNOW what Dag saw in Simon. It has to be more than just being college friends. Look at all the crap Simon pulled on him. He slept with his wife and then married her after Dag divorced her. He can't be clean. There's too much money involved. Dag moved two billion dollars in assets to charities over Thanksgiving weekend. But Simon isn't hurting for cash. He blew up his own plane and was able to get from Cuba to Croatia with new ID and no financial hardship. Angel owns this villa—read that 'mansion'—and I'm sure she's got a couple of million stashed away for retirement.

I finally hauled my ass out of bed about eight-thirty. I considered calling Cinnamon but either she was in bed or thinking about who she was going to get there. I took a shower and stood wrapped in a towel looking out at the sea. I can see the ferry dock from here. A ferry came in while I was watching and I could see people getting off.

My mind kept playing tricks on me. I kept thinking I could see people I knew. I saw a guy with a cane and a limp and thought Jordan was there. I'd have sworn I saw Cinnamon, Geoff Gilliam, Brenda, Bradley, Oksamma, Ray, and one time even Dag. I suppose I'll be seeing ghosts till the day I die and join them.

┤ ┼ ┼ ┼ ┼╫╫╫┼┼ ┼ ┼ ┼ ├

COFFEE WASN'T BAD at all. When I got downstairs and found the kitchen, Angel was the only one there. Simon was staying on the third floor and decided it was best to stay out of sight for a while. Apparently, my warning was being considered. What he could do about it, though, I really didn't know. I had no intention of getting between him and whoever Brenda was sending after him. I figured it was no one I knew, so what good was I really. If I'd had Angel's phone number, I could have saved myself a trip and a lot of sleepless hours.

How could I have been so stupid as to think because I managed to hide out in the Condo a few days, Brenda and her executive groupies would consider me any kind of threat? I assessed the sum of what I knew and what I figured they knew about me.

They knew Angel gave the thumb drive to Dag and I probably had it. They'd ransacked my office when I disappeared. They didn't find it or me.

They knew James Whitcomb camped out at the Condo a few days. I'd dumped Davy in the hot tub when I left but I was pretty sure no one knew Deb Riley was James Whitcomb.

Someone knew James Whitcomb had done business with Angel and then disappeared a few days later.

Finally, they knew Angel had this property in Croatia.

Unless they had something else, it wasn't much to go on. I'd given Jordan more information than that. As far as I could figure, none of the Committee knew anything about me or that I was with Angel now or that I was James Whitcomb.

I'd book a flight home and send the original thumb drive to Brenda's address. My name would be wiped off their list of naughty and nice. They'd never know I'd sent all the data to Jordan.

After Angel greeted me, she had coffee ready in a flash. She had this great machine you punch a button on, it grinds the coffee, and brews a beautiful cup of rich black joe. I gotta get me one of those. She said in the US they cost about $1,500!

Maybe I'll just hire Jackie, the barista at Tovoni's to hand deliver a cup every day!

"So, what are you going to do, Angel?" I asked. She started to whimper and I saw a tear in her eye.

"We were up half the night. We should run but Simon thinks he did the wrong thing coming here. If they come here, we stand a chance. This place is pretty defensible. If we run… well, it wouldn't be hard to spot a five-nine man with a six-foot blonde. I don't know. I'm scared but I don't want to leave him."

I could sympathize a little. Simon had eight powerful enemies and probably more knowledge about what was happening in their world than anyone else. I bet Jordan wished he had Simon on the witness stand instead of just having a disk full of names and accounts.

Barbarian at the gate

"Angel," I said out of the blue as we were having toast, "I want to know more about your business. You had FinCEN and the FBI hanging around your shop before you left. They were watching everybody who came in or out. What is it you really do?"

"Financial Crimes Enforcement? They're always hanging around. They've been trying to pin a money laundering scheme on me for months. I'm not worried about them unless they send in the VICE squad. Now that would be embarrassing."

"But you are, aren't you?" I asked.

"Laundering money? No. I don't think so. There's nothing illegal about hiding your money. You can hide it under your mattress if you want to. I convert it to instruments that can be hidden more easily. Any cash transaction of more than $5,000, I dutifully report on my little form. They know I can't possibly handle the kind of cash they want to investigate."

"What about these?" I asked, tossing one of my cash cards on the table in front of her.

"How did you get one of these?" she asked picking it up. "It's just a cash card. You can buy them at the bank. If you don't put more than $5,000 on it in a cash transaction, there's nothing stopping you from buying it and using it anyplace in the world. Now, come on. Which shop did you get this one in? It's from our network."

"Yours." I pulled out the other card from my wallet. "You charge a pretty hefty commission to fill one up."

Angel looked at me strangely and closely. I stared her straight in the eye. She slowly began to grin.

"The little gay college professor? You?" I nodded. "I can't believe it. You said you could disguise yourself so we'd never recognize you. That was incredible! Have you done Cinnamon and Teri yet?" I nodded.

"Let's get back to the question," I said. "You ran this as two different transactions and took a twenty percent commission on the deal. That totaled $12,000. But you didn't report it. Isn't that a little contrary to the law?"

"If you were picky enough, maybe. But it still isn't money laundering."

"It sure isn't a service offered by most travel agents."

"I handled about $1.5 million a year," Angel said. "Simon got me the business and introduced me to people a long time ago. But there isn't anything illegal about what I do."

"It's still too shady," Simon said from the doorway. "I never should have gotten you into this. They all know you helped them hide money from their wives. They'll all be afraid of you." He looked pretty worn this morning and Angel jumped up to kiss him. She made coffee and had him at the table with us in seconds. So domestic. "What you have there, Miss Riley, is the contemporary equivalent of a bearer bond. You can't get those in the US anymore. You can in some countries, but if you're caught transporting them into the US, the government will confiscate it if you don't declare it and tax it if you do. Detecting a few extra credit cards is much harder to do. There are a lot of men and a few women who have no difficulty withdrawing a few thousand dollars in miscellaneous funds from joint checking accounts. Their spouses don't even notice it, probably because they are also withdrawing similar amounts. It's their insurance money, paid in advance. They convert little stashes of cash to gift cards. That's also completely legal. You can even put more on the same card later. It's instant cash, anyplace in the world. So, a business executive on a trip for two weeks in Asia with no wife and fear of a sexual harassment suit from his secretary, can't even approach someone on the street because he could be recognized. But he can go online and pick his favorite escort, have him or her at his room for the night and gone before he meets his coworkers for breakfast. The escort is paid with untraceable funds that he pulled from the local ATM on the way back to his hotel. There's no personal information contained on that card. If you have the card and the PIN, you have the money. He paid for his night with an A-class model with money he stuck in his pocket months ago. It's the closest thing we have to fully anonymous banking."

"You can't tell me Angel brings in $1.5 million a year in money executives spend on hookers," I spat. Sorry, Angel, but let's call it what it is.

"Lots of reasons to hide money. Divorce in your future? Want to ride a spaceship? Need to pay off a gambling debt? Want to move your assets to a nice safe Swiss bank account where your children will be able to get it after you die without paying estate taxes on it? Carry a hundred thou in cash on each of your trips to Europe and you'll raise a flag. Carry five $20,000 cash cards and no one will ever know."

"So, the difference between this and money laundering is what?" I asked. "Step one is convert the funds into a negotiable instrument. Taking fifty $20s and having them give you back ten $100s. Yeah that's small potatoes. But you're taking fifty $100s and giving them one little plastic $5,000 bill. It's the same thing."

"If it weren't so profitable, we'd have gotten out of the business a long time ago. Twenty percent commission on the sale. All declared. Taxes paid. For every $100,000 you manage to hide, we get $20,000. Better than the stock market and we move everything into our own foreign accounts. Right now, all we're trying to do is retire. There are money launderers out there who work two orders of magnitude above the business we do. Those are the guys FinCEN is interested in. It just happens FinCEN is mad at me because I didn't give them the data I promised. I gave it to Dag instead and you broke into it and decided to become a vigilante—go after them yourself. You're way out of your league on this one, babe. I just need to stay holed up until that cop I cut the deal with cools off and uses the data on that disk you cracked. Please tell me you gave it to Dag's friend, Jordan Grant."

"You know Jordan?"

"He's the cop I cut the deal with months ago. I promised to give him evidence of a massive fraud collaborated on by Seattle's top execs."

"WTF!" I grabbed my phone and sent a one-hand text message to Jordan: 'What do you want me to do with Simon Barnett?' I didn't expect an answer very soon. It was two o'clock in the morning in Seattle. "So how did you discover this massive fraud?" I asked.

"My wife and I have been spying on each other for years. That was what led to the ugly affair that broke up Dag's marriage and saddled me with mine," Simon said. "She was already brokering deals with local businessmen and politicians, way back then. I bought her the Condo years ago, when they first started renovating that area. It became the place she used to bring the players to the table."

"No one could see them come or go and no surveillance was allowed," I said. "I watched it in action."

"She always had a supply of hostesses who were happy to dress nicely and work for 'tips.' When I realized she was pushing the limits close to having an operating brothel in Seattle, I stepped in and started enforcing standards on behavior and conduct. I won't say sex never takes place at the Condo, but I used it more as an employment agency. I found beautiful intelligent young women and put them in a place where they could be discovered. They had one-on-one chats with men they would never get to talk to, even if they worked for the same company. Those men, in turn, used their influence to get the women jobs in their companies. Those jobs were always equivalent to what any man with the same education and experience could have gotten by walking in off the street."

"How altruistic."

"It was one of the things the men agreed to. Sponsor a woman in the Condo and set her up with a good employer. Never mess with an employee. Find good women. The mentor was responsible for seeing the woman learned how to get the most they could from a job. The men in the Condo got to spend time with beautiful young women.

"So, you want me to believe the Condo is just a place where a few lucky young women are given a better chance at good jobs and isn't a place where rich men go to get laid."

"That's a little harsh, Deb," Angel broke in. "You can't judge all the girls at the Condo by me. I'm a professional girlfriend—or I was until Simon came along."

"You didn't become an amateur, baby," Simon said, giving her a squeeze. I thought back to my experiences at the Condo. I'd been a recruit, a hostage, and a manager. I had to admit, even Cinnamon was happy with what she was doing. I was going to have some long talks with that girl when I got back to town. She couldn't work for me and work at the Condo.

My cellphone vibrated and I walked into the next room to look at it. I had a message from Jordan. That was fast! 'Protect him if you can but don't risk yourself. We're pulling them in and I have a warrant for BB. Be careful!'

I shoved the phone in my pocket as I looked out the living room window. Down at the front gate I could see a man looking up at the house. This time I wasn't imagining everyone I knew getting off the ferry. This time I was sure. Geoff Gilliam was in Croatia.

———|—+++++++||||||||++++++|———

It took about ten minutes to convince Angel and Simon things were serious. When I told them who it was, Simon was convinced he had to move. Geoff Gilliam had a reputation as a sadist at the Condo. In my experience, his presence just meant there were thugs around. Both Cinnamon and Teri had confirmed he was all talk and no action in private. But I'd seen the kind of people around him, including that bitch bodyguard, Savon. If Brenda was picking his travel companions, none of us were safe.

My counterplot was hatched over dinner. I needed hair dye. Why was I not surprised that Simon just happened to have a men's hair color product on hand? As black as his hair was, I was surprised there was any left.

I got Simon to give me the passport he'd used to get into the country and graciously supplied him with James Whitcomb's in trade. Then I went to work. I gave my short red wig to Angel and had her dye it black and blow it dry. *Damn!* I liked that wig but Riley Finn was a dead alias. It would take me months to build a new one. I pulled together the remnants of the beard and eyebrows I used for James Whitcomb and used the fringe of hair to create a full closely cropped beard like Simon's. I pulled out my man-suit and padded the old chest again. Then I restyled the now-black wig into a more manly cut. I dressed and looked in the mirror. I glanced at the passport picture. I'd pass.

When I went downstairs, Simon's reaction was completely different. He didn't care about the hair and beard but complained that he wasn't that fat and my suit looked like I got it out of a secondhand shop. Which was true. He disappeared and returned with a different set of clothes from his own wardrobe. He might say he wasn't that fat but the clothes fit. Designer label clothes with his initials embroidered on the cuffs. Tailored clothes for sailing. What a prick.

I have to say, once that I put it on, I really liked it. I might want to keep wearing it for a while. Cinnamon would love this.

—————— +—+—+—+ + ++++++++++ + +—+—— ——————

I'VE REPACKED, LIGHTLY. I keep buying clothes and leaving them behind. All I needed were the essentials it would take for me to change back to Deb Riley. It's time to flee another country. How routine is this becoming? I didn't even have a chance to decide if I like Croatia.

{26}
The crossing

WASHINGTON CROSSED THE DELAWARE, we're told, on Christmas Eve, 1776. Maybe the next day, I don't remember. My Christmas Eve will be spent crossing the Adriatic Sea. Washington's rowboats had a mile to traverse. I have about 100 miles. At least I have a motor.

Help arrives

IT WAS SUPPOSED to be a simple ruse. Anyone watching the house would think Simon left the country. I'd be dressed like him and catch the ferry to Split and a plane to Rome as Simon. Somewhere en route, I'd change from Simon to Deb and catch a flight from Rome home. Anyone watching would be following me long enough that Simon and Angel could sneak out and start over anyplace they wanted to. End of case. I wash my hands.

But when I got downstairs last night, Angel had her bags packed and ready to go with me. The two of them convinced me it would be more believable if Angel and Simon escaped together. They're a recognizable pair with the statuesque blonde Angel towering over the short dark Simon.

We planned to leave in the middle of the night and instead of taking the ferry, take their boat up the inland passage to Rijeka and drive to Zagreb from there. Along the way, I'd lose the disguise and two blondes would grab a car to Zagreb and a plane home. While we were luring away our pursuers, Simon would disappear south to Greece and lay low a couple of months. As soon as things were safe, he'd call for Angel to join him.

"Well, I'll be go-to-hell," I said mimicking Simon's favorite oath. Both Angel and Simon snapped a startled look at me.

"You sound more like Simon than Simon does," Angel said. "This could be a fun trip."

Simon growled a little about having too much fun. It was still a risky endeavor. The toughest part would be getting from the house down to the dock. Once we were in the boat, it would take someone with a boat to catch up to us. The ferries didn't run at night. We'd be long gone by morning. We haggled back and forth for a good hour before everyone was agreed on a plan that would get us all away from the immediate danger of Geoff Gilliam and crew.

The goodbye kiss between Angel and Simon made my stomach ache.

It was close to two in the morning when Angel and I carried our one suitcase each out of the house, looking in all directions and heading down to the wharf. Simon gave me an overcoat to wear as well, even though he knew I'd be ditching the suit and coat before we debarked.

I handed my suitcase to Angel and she started the big diesel engines while I tossed the lines onto the boat and jumped aboard. I was relieved to see it was a 30' Four Winds 288 Vista Cruiser and not a rowboat. It was a luxury yacht made to accommodate two people for fast trips to Greece, Italy, or any other port on the Mediterranean.

Angel didn't hear me hit the deck over the sound of the engines. I was shoved and fell next to the suitcases. I rolled to my knees facing a gun.

"Hello, Simon," Ray growled. "Going somewhere?" At that moment, Angel looked back and screamed. I thought Ray was going to shoot her. "Both of you! Get down below and shut up."

"There's no need to be so nasty, Ray," I said. "It's good to see you, too."

"Right," he said. "I'll take the boat from here. Just get below and don't either of you stick your head out before I tell you. There's no reason for a lot of people to get hurt."

Pretty gruff if you ask me. The Ray Hawkins I'd met on Ambergris Caye seemed more easy going. I wondered if Geoff was making things difficult. Or maybe he was pissed because I gave him the slip in Mexico

City at the airport. Well, if he was working for Jordan, that would explain why he'd been following me. Good old Jordan, still looking out for me.

"Aye, aye, Captain Bligh," I said beneath my breath, ushering Angel below deck with our suitcases. "It's okay, Angel. Jordan said I'd recognize the guy he sent to help. It's a relief."

Ray closed the door when we'd entered the forward cabin. There was shouting from the dock and I heard angry voices and running feet. Ray gunned the engines and the boat lurched from the pier with G-force acceleration. Angel and I fell onto the bed together and clutched each other out of fright. We stayed that way for several minutes, trying to listen for sounds of pursuit but hearing nothing but the slap of the waves and rumble of the engines as we sped across the channel separating us from Split.

"Geoff must have been close," I whispered as we finally sat up and separated. "Thank God Ray got here when he did."

The devil and the deep blue

IT SEEMED LIKE we'd been down there forever.

"How long is the crossing from Brac to Split?" I asked Angel.

"Less than an hour. Maybe he's using the same plan we came up with and going up to Rijeka."

"I'm glad someone is piloting the boat who knows how to handle it."

"I know how," Angel said. "Simon and I have had this boat for two years. I can handle it just fine."

"Well, let's find out where we are," I said, opening my computer. It's a great thing to have a GPS receiver in a laptop. Dag was smart about that. I waited for the map to resolve and an indicator that the GPS had acquired a signal. When it did, I stood up, hit my head on the low ceiling, and fell back into the bed.

"This isn't right," I said. "We're not headed up the coast." I pointed to the screen. We'd come through the narrow straight between Brac and Solta islands and were headed southeast—out to sea.

I tried to open the door, only to discover it was locked from outside.

"Hey! Ray!" I yelled. "Where do you think we're going?"

"Keep your head inside or I'll blow it off!" he yelled back. WTF??? I sat with Angel and we watched the blip on the map that showed us headed out into the Adriatic see. We were definitely headed for the Mediterranean if he continued this direction. I grabbed my cellphone and tried to call Jordan but we were already too far out to get a signal. Next time I go chasing around the world, I'll get a Sat phone. It was time for two girls to start looking for ways to defend ourselves.

Angel knew everything stored on the boat and had harpoons and scuba gear on the bed in no time. I couldn't see what the point was with the scuba gear. I wasn't going diving. The harpoon definitely held possibilities, though. The only problem was it was so long that by the time I could get it positioned to use, Ray could easily blow me away. I was always better at defensive maneuvers than at figuring out how to attack someone. I stowed a knife in my belt and decided that would be the extent of my weaponry.

I checked the GPS and saw we were passing the Island of Vis but there was still no signal on my phone. Well, we were as prepared as we could be. Angel and I lay cuddled together on the bed waiting. I guess we dozed off because I came suddenly awake and alert to the silence of the powerful twin engines. I glanced at the GPS again and saw we were halfway to Italy. The map showed nothing but blue.

The water was rough and the waves were slapping against the side of the boat. We could hear Ray scraping things around above deck. Then he yelled at us.

"I'm opening the door! Stand back." The door jiggled and opened just wide enough for Ray to see we weren't waiting to jump him. "Get out here, Simon," he yelled, backing up with the gun still trained on the stairs. I stepped out and saw Angel glancing toward the harpoon on the bed. There was no way she could get to it with him pointing a gun at us.

"Close and lock the door then get up here on deck." I looked at the lock on the door as I pulled it closed. Angel ran forward and held the door just before it latched.

"You're making a big mistake, Ray," I said as I emerged from the hold. "Jordan said you'd help me."

"I don't know a Jordan," Ray said. "The orders from your loving wife are to make sure when you're lost at sea this time, you stay lost."

I looked at Ray. How could I have been so wrong about him? He wasn't sent by Jordan to help me. He was the assassin sent by Brenda to finish off Simon. How could I have been so stupid?

"Come on, move. Over there." He waved his gun toward the stern. I moved back. At least that would put his back to the door of the cabin. If Angel could sneak out, maybe she could surprise him. "Now jump," he commanded.

"No," I said. "You're making a mistake Ray. I'm not Simon. I'm Deb Riley. You helped me escape from Belize."

"Nice try, Simon. We figured she was working with you before we ever set her up at the party. We figured she'd lead us right to you. She gave me the slip in Mexico City, but that's when I figured out Riley Finn and Deb Riley were the same person. The beauty is, she thinks I'm the good guy and I can use her when I get back stateside."

"I'm Deb," I said. He was already raising his gun. The SOB was going to shoot me!

"Jump or we do it the old-fashioned way."

"No." I could see his hand tightening on the gun and knew that was the last thing I was ever going to see. A wave hit the boat and it lurched to the side. I lost my footing. I grabbed the rail and fell to the deck. I saw Ray stumble toward me, the gun still pointed my direction. Then, as if in slow motion, he kept stumbling forward and over the end rail of the boat into the choppy water. A harpoon was stuck through his back.

Angel was standing in the doorway of the cabin staring out at the sea.

"Angel," I said.

"Sorry it took so long," she responded. "I had to be sure he wasn't watching the door."

"I'm so sorry, Angel."

"He was trying to kill Simon. I couldn't let that happen," she said. "I've already lost him too many times."

I went to her and hugged her tightly. She turned back to the wheelhouse.

"Get your GPS while I get the engines started," she said. "We need to plot a course that gets us home."

We used the computer GPS to get a broader look at where we were while Angel used the boat's GPS to plot a course. We chose Pescara, Italy as the closest friendly port.

"We've been there before. They have a beautiful little marina," she said. It was midmorning when we docked and Angel made arrangements to leave the boat for a month. She expects to be back soon. I looked back at the boat as we were leaving and realized anyone could have been waiting for us on Brac. The back of the boat was emblazoned in bright letters, "Angel."

———————+—+++++⊪⊪⊪+++++—+———————

WE CAUGHT A train at the Stazione Centrale di Pescara and headed north. Once we got into a private cabin, I stripped and changed out of my Simon Barnett clothes. I decided I was going to stay Deb Riley for a while.

I should get in touch with Jordan but I need to pick up an Italian SIM for my phone. I'm wiped out. I'll do it at the next stop, after I sleep for a while. Angel's making flight arrangements to get us home. It's been an exhausting Christmas Eve.

{27}
Homesick

I'M NOT SURE WHERE I AM. I woke up about seven and we're still on the train. I know we changed trains someplace in Switzerland last night, so I suppose we're in France. Angel said she booked us home from Amsterdam. Home. That's all I care about right now. I just want to go curl up in my very own bed and sleep for about a month.

———+—+—+—+++II||||I|I|+—+—+—+———

Christmas gifts

WE ROLLED INTO Paris about nine to change trains to Amsterdam. I'm glad I'm traveling with Angel. She knows where everything is and where to get the best shopping deals on Christmas morning. She's been really down. I understand… well, as much as I can. She killed Ray Hawkins.

I can't even begin to say how thankful I am. That's twice in two months I've stared down the barrel of a gun. That's twice too often.

I wanted to get something for Angel but had no idea what. The girl either has or could get anything she wanted. The shops here sell everything from Givenchy to Valrhona. I decided to keep it simple. Then we headed for the Eurostar to Amsterdam.

———+—+—+—+++II||||I|I|+—+—+—+———

WE GOT A decent connection to Schiphol Airport. I sent a text to Jordan on the train. Short and sweet. "Jordan. I'm coming home. Hawkins lost at sea. Angel with me. Simon presumed safe. WTF with Gilliam?"

I haven't heard back, not that I expect much.

The Eurostar is fast but not all that comfortable. The motion affected me worse than the boat in rough water across the Adriatic. Maybe I just had too much adrenalin pumping on the boat to notice. I managed to hold my bread and cheese and complimentary glass of champagne down.

"Merry Christmas, Angel," I said, handing her the hastily purchased and wrapped gift. Her eyes lit up. I guess that's the real secret. She can buy almost anything she wants but she likes to be spoiled. Any gift is exciting. She unwrapped the black silk scarf. It has a pattern of interlinked hands embroidered around the edge in scarlet. It's clear they are all women's hands.

"This is beautiful, Deb," she said. "I love it."

"We blondes gotta stick together," I said. She looked a little strangely at me. Yeah, it's just a wig. Then she surprised me by handing me a package as well. I unwrapped the present and almost cried. It was a turban wrap like we'd seen many women wearing in Europe. It's a beautiful dark blue with silver piping. If I wanted to, I could probably wear it out without wearing a wig. We haven't talked much about it but Angel figured out that when I dressed as a bald man, I was really bald.

"I don't know about you," she said, "but a lot of times I don't want to bother getting my hair all fixed just to go out for coffee. These turbans are so stylish and no one can tell if you've washed your hair and spent an hour drying it or if you just shaved it all off."

"Thank you, Angel," I said.

"Hey," she answered, "we blondes gotta stick together."

I stopped at Duty Free to pick up a gift for Cinnamon. Simple. I don't want her to get any inappropriate ideas. I don't think. Text from Jordan said, "Good work. I'll meet you at the airport." Hmm. Maybe I should get him a gift, too.

I called Cinnamon just before flight time. It's a nine-hour time change, so only seven thirty in the morning there.

"Merry Christmas!" I said when she answered.

"Not unless you're coming home," she said. "I don't have anyone to celebrate with."

"Angel and I are both on our way. Can you stand having us all together?"

"As long as we're not going to the Condo. Maybe I can get Teri to come over, too. It will be like we started the month," she said.

"Right. You can all pay me the bets you owe me."

"We'll have dinner at your apartment," she said. "I'll take care of everything. Do you want me to meet you at the airport? I've got this classy Mustang polished and ready to roll."

"I've got a ride," I said. "You should plan on a couple more for dinner, which means we'll need to eat with plates on our laps. Is anything open where you can get food? We could just order Chinese."

"Leave it to me, Sugar," she said. "Your dog will be here, too. She hasn't left me alone for the past four days."

"You have Maizie?" I exclaimed. "How's my baby doing?"

"Oh, we get along just fine. She's staked out her own space in the office and I went to Petco and bought her a new bed. She loves it. Mrs. Prior dropped her off Friday and said, 'Maizie is too concerned about Deb to stay with me. She wants to be here when Deb gets home.' Mrs. Prior is a hoot."

"If Maizie starts talking to you, too, I want to know about it," I laughed. "God, I'm looking forward to being home. I think this case is wrapped up."

"Um... Don't count on that, Sugar. I can't tell what's happening but something is up. There was a little article in Saturday's paper that says Belize authorities detained an American citizen on drug charges. Reportedly from the Seattle area. Federal agents indicate they have no records of the detainee and have dispatched an agent to meet with officials in Belize City. That's all. It's one of those short article things on the second page of the International News. It stuck out when I read it because you were just there. It might have something to do with the case."

"You're going to make a detective yet," I said. "I'm betting it was meant for a very few important people to see. I've got to board now. I'll see you in a few hours."

"See you soon, Sugar. Be safe."

I'm going to like having Cinnamon around.

———————|—+—+—+—+—++|||||||++—+—+—+——

Surprise at SeaTac

I SLEPT A lot of the flight home. We were treated like royalty in First Class.

Or I guess it's called Business Class. Feels like First Class to me. We had an on-time arrival, which Angel says means we got to SeaTac within an hour of when we were supposed to. Since we were in the front of the plane, we were the first ones to Passport Control.

That's when everything started to fall apart. The agent looked hard at my passport and asked me some strange questions about where I'd been. I only had one stamp, indicating my arrival in the European Union. Well, officially, that's the only place I'd been.

He motioned an officer over and I knew I was well and truly busted. A line of coach class passengers behind me was getting fidgety. Next thing I knew, I was being led away from Passport Control by a man in uniform with a gun who had a firm grip on my left arm with one hand and my passport with the other. I could hear the rhythmic clicking of Angel's heels as she was escorted behind me.

We were put in separate rooms and the officer left, telling me to please wait quietly. I was surprised he left me with my rollaboard bag, containing my computer. I looked at my cellphone to see if I could text Jordan but there was no signal in the room.

After about ten minutes of fidgeting on the cold metal chair, the door opened again and Jordan Grant walked in. I should say, hobbled in. He had a cast on one leg and moved with a crutch.

"Jordan!" I said in relief. I started to get up but he held out a hand to stop me.

"Deborah H. Riley," he said in a monotone. I was no longer relieved to see him. "What have we here? Fleeing an arrest warrant. False identity. Forgery, theft, computer crime, concealing negotiable currency, I can't tell you how many penalties there are for possessing a false US Passport. What else can we add? Murder? Kidnapping?"

"Jordan! You know that's not true. You've known where I was all along and what I was doing. You told me that guy was there to help me, not to kill me. You said I was doing a good job!"

"Shit, Deb. That's why I'm here instead of letting Homeland Security intercept you. I swore out warrants for both you and Angel Woodward so we could intercept you when you got off the plane instead of letting Customs find whatever you might have in your baggage. I've got an officer collecting your luggage and as soon as he lets me know, we'll get you two out of here. Until then, you're under arrest."

"Geez, Jordan," I gasped. "You scared me."

"As you should be scared," he answered. "Both for the past and the future."

"What do you mean?"

"The best I've been able to put things together, you found out about a warrant for your arrest that was never actually sworn out. The only place it was mentioned was in your office, so you must have a way of listening in to what happens there without being detected. You adopted a disguise and identity—a very good one, by the way—and hid out in a place you could hack into the customs and immigration control of half a dozen different countries. You assaulted a guard at a certain condo and threw him off a roof, fortunately into a hot tub. Davy, by the way, has decided security is not really his calling. Oh, and the forged documents leasing that condo. You used your false identity to get cash cards from a less than reputable source under investigation by FinCEN. You used a forged passport to enter another country where you apparently changed identities again. You trespassed on property you had no business being near, chased down a fugitive from FinCEN in Croatia, and evaded the help I sent for you. What the hell happened in the Adriatic where Simon Barnett and Angel Woodward escaped with known felon and suspected assassin, Ray Hawkins, I have no idea. But Simon entered Italy under one of his known aliases and disappeared. But lo and behold, Deb Riley was suddenly traveling in the company of Angel. Did I miss anything?"

"Yes, but it's not worth mentioning," I sighed. "That's the past. Okay, I'm scared. What's the future?"

"Eight angry executives want your head." I groaned. That was just what I needed. With luck, Jordan would take me to prison.

"I thought you'd arrest them! I sent you all that evidence Simon provided."

"Do you have any idea what would happen to the local, regional, and maybe national economy if I arrested executives from eight major corporations in Seattle and accused them all of fraud and embezzlement? Think what happened when the Enron execs were arrested. Multiply it by eight!"

"You're not going to do anything? All that was wasted effort?"

"I didn't say we weren't doing anything. I said I couldn't make arrests. We're having one on one meetings with the Committee. Some of them are remarkably forthcoming about what they were doing, as if they couldn't believe there was anything illegal about it."

"That sounds like Reinholdt. He figures it's his money and he can do what he wants with it."

"Others are reluctant to tell tales out of school, as it were. They're still looking for ways to cover their tracks."

"Gilliam," I supplied. "He was covering tracks all the way to Croatia."

"Oh, you'd be surprised about that one. If you'd stayed put in either Belize or Croatia, he'd have gotten you to safety."

"What?!" I couldn't believe my ears. "That sadistic playboy?"

"A rich playboy sports team owner gets bored. Being approached to do undercover work for the government is a thrill. And we didn't even have to pay his expenses. I arranged to have him take your friend Teri with him to Belize under the mistaken opinion she'd recognize you. Geoff had his suspicions when you came up with a bug at the dinner party but Teri confirmed them when she suddenly got sick and followed you to the boat. He was quite distraught when he discovered you'd both escaped. When we found out from Teri about you going with Ray Hawkins, you sent us into a panic. Thank you for at least using your own name and passport to fly from Mexico to Croatia. I got Geoff on a plane to intercept you."

"My head's spinning," I said. There was a light rap on the door and it opened to a guy in a suit.

"We're ready." Jordan turned to me and fastened my left wrist to his right with handcuffs.

"Time to head for the car," he said. I still pulled my bag while he used his other hand to manipulate his cane and bum leg. In the hall, another officer was leading Angel into a network of tunnels to an underground garage. Two cars were waiting. I was a little ticked that he didn't let Angel and me ride together but he followed me into the back seat with the cuffs still in place.

Being cuffed wrist-to-wrist doesn't leave a lot of options open as to where you can put your hands. I didn't really think much of it when Jordan put his hand on mine. When we were out of the airport and on the highway, however, he leaned over and whispered to me.

"I was worried about you, Deb." He squeezed my hand and unlocked the cuffs.

WTF?

{28}
The never-ending story

MORE PEOPLE ARE DEPRESSED at Christmas than any other time of the year. I get it. I catch myself thinking, "When I see Dag…" or "I need to tell Dag…" But Dag isn't there. I don't know what I'd do if I didn't have friends.

Almost homeless

"MERRY CHRISTMAS," CINNAMON said, lingering as she kissed me on the cheek when I entered the room. I noticed she spent considerably less effort on her peck on Angel's cheek and somewhat more on Jordan. One of the other officers brought all our luggage up and told Jordan he'd be available whenever. Maizie came running to me, sniffed up one leg and down the other and decided I was okay. She stood on her hind legs until I knelt down on the floor to pet her.

I looked around my apartment trying to remember when I was last here. At first all I noticed was holiday decorations. Then I noticed the 'tree' was made of cardboard boxes. I started to tell Cinnamon it was very creative when I realized my things weren't in their usual places. In fact, they weren't anywhere. I know I left in a hurry but I didn't strip the apartment.

"Cinnamon," I said, "what's going on?"

"Honey you forgot," she answered. "With all that's happened the past two months, you probably haven't even looked at your mail. Your lease is up. The manager came by while I was here last week and handed me an eviction notice. Apparently, they're redoing the apartments in this building and turning them into condos. It's a big thing now."

"I'm being evicted? What am I supposed to do? I won't go!"

"Sure you will, Honey. You've got that other little apartment. I met your landlady, Mrs. Prior, when she brought Maizie over a few days ago. The first thing she asked was when you were moving into the apartment. I told her it looked like the end of the month. I thought I'd get a head start for you and pack."

There was too much going on for me to process, but geez! I go away for a few days and my whole life is changed. That wasn't the end of the news. Teri was there and we hugged each other and started talking at once about how worried we were about each other. In the midst of our giggles of relief, she stopped and turned all serious on me.

"Deb, I've got a new boyfriend!" she blurted out.

"No way!" I said. "Why didn't you bring him over. We're having a party."

"I invited him," she said, "but I told him he couldn't come in until you agreed."

"Why not?" There was a knock on the door and I turned to answer it.

"Because you really need to give him permission to enter your home." I pulled the door open and almost slammed it back shut in the face of Geoff Gilliam. I turned to Teri with my mouth hanging open to my knees.

"Him?" I said. Teri nodded. My best friend was dating a member of the Committee—okay, maybe an undercover federal agent on the Committee—who was a reputed playboy, sadist, and womanizer. I turned back to the door.

"Miss Riley," he said. "I'm glad to officially meet you. I'm sorry if we got off on the wrong foot the first time."

"Come in, Mr. Gilliam," I said formally. "But if you are going to date my best friend, could we please call each other by our first names. I'm Deb."

"I'm Geoff," he responded with a smile. Killer smile. Poor Teri. "Pleased to meet you." He stepped into the room and Teri caught him in a lip-lock that made the rest of us turn away to give them privacy.

"Well, merry Christmas, everybody," I said, "and God bless us all."

"Come to the tables, everybody," Cinnamon called. She must have gotten card tables and chairs from everyone she knew. "The chef says he's ready to serve."

"Chef?" I asked. "Who now?" The question was answered as my advisor Lars Andersen walked in from the kitchen with a huge turkey on a platter. "Lars!" I exclaimed and rushed to hug him as soon as he'd set the turkey down.

"Merry Christmas, Riley," he said.

Over dinner, Angel and I were called upon to relate our story. It was helped along by Jordan, Cinnamon, Teri, and Geoff all adding bits about their parts. The puzzle pieces all seemed to fit together somehow but Angel and I carefully avoided details about how Ray Hawkins departed from this world. We'll talk to Jordan about it but no one needs to know Angel shot him with a harpoon. We just said he fell overboard and we didn't see him again.

———————

With Brenda Barnett in a Belize jail on drug running charges under a pseudonym the US Government won't recognize and the Committee all agreeing to make restitution, it's beginning to sound like my first case is wrapped up nice and tidy. I have to finish packing and then go to inspect my office before I start moving things over to Dag's apartment.

Will I ever think of it as my apartment? Or is the whole life I'm living just a continuation of his? I've got to do some serious thinking.

———————

New office

OMG! It's beautiful. I got to the office this morning and Cinnamon was sitting behind a new desk where my old desk used to be. The walls have been painted a soft green. There are plants and a new rug.

Then I walked into Dag's office. My office now. Cinnamon is amazing. The place is unbelievable. The pieces of furniture are generally smaller than Dag's furniture was. It's sleek and modern with lots of glass. Maizie came in with me and went trotting over to the girliest little bed you've ever seen. She was so proud of it!

There's no place to hide anything. My desk is wide open with nothing more enclosed than a pencil drawer. On it was the remote control for the new 52-inch plasma TV screen that hangs on the opposite wall. The old remote sat beside it.

And pictures. She brought some of my photos from the apartment and put them on my desk. The one of Dag and me at Pier 57 sits by itself on one side of the table. I'll keep that one here. I don't know how to tell Cinnamon the others are all fakes.

I was never photographed much as a child. My mother burned any photos she could find and I kept my little stash well-hidden. The family pictures, even my parents' wedding picture, are all fake. They are all pictures of me in various disguises.

When I was little, I could never pass one of those little photo kiosks without getting my picture taken. My father would indulge me with a dollar and keep Mom occupied while I got my treasures. It meant I had a lot of pictures of me clowning around, smiling, serious, and what have you. But they didn't have any background. So, I scanned all the pictures, looked up photos of different scenery on the Internet, and airbrushed myself into them in a digital editing program. It worked so well for my childhood photos, I started taking pictures of myself in disguise and brushing them into the photos as my parents.

I got pretty good at digital editing. You have to look really closely in order to tell they aren't completely natural and right. Cinnamon chose some of my best work. My parents' wedding picture, the three of us at the Grand Canyon (never actually been there), and my graduation picture. Maybe I'll leave them here after all.

Cinnamon closed the door between our offices and left me alone.

I stood by the window looking out over Puget Sound and thought about the past two months. It seems my whole world changed the day Brenda Barnett brought Simon's laptop into Dag's office. I've been going for fifty-seven days now, thinking about all the crap she pulled. I'm no longer at a desk in the outer office working on my thesis with Dag humming away in here. All Dag's furniture is gone and I'm standing by his window with stupid tears running down my cheeks and Maizie standing next to me, leaning against my leg.

I sat down on the sofa and Maizie jumped up on my lap. I buried my face in her fur and cried.

━━━┼━┼┼┼┼┼╫╫╫╫┼┼┼┼━┼━

Hungry lioness on the loose

I GOT A call from Jordan while I was trying to sort things out in my office. He said he'd like to hire me to do an analysis of how they were pulling off the mobile phone scam. I can do that. What I didn't figure out while I was still holed up at the Condo, Simon filled in when I was in Croatia. Jordan also says he needs a bill from me for my services cracking the encryption on Simon's computer. I can't bill him for the field work because, officially, I wasn't working for him. But I can bill him a lot of time 'at Dag's old rates' for the computer work. That's good because I've got to pay for redecorating the office and figure out a salary for Cinnamon. She says Lars submitted insurance claims on behalf of the estate and most of the new stuff should be covered.

"Oh, by the way," Jordan said casually, "Brenda has escaped from Belize."

WTF???

"I thought she was in jail where the sun would never shine and the government wasn't going to help her," I exclaimed.

"That's a problem with working with a government that's mostly not corrupt but isn't strong enough to enforce its own laws," he said. "In a really corrupt government, we could have spread some money around to the right people and the problem would have been solved permanently."

"You wouldn't!"

"No, of course not. I'm just saying we could make sure things stayed the way we wanted them to," he said. "The problem with an honest government is they would be highly offended by any suggestion that they do something not as respectable as they consider themselves. So, we can't make any offers at a level that can enforce the agreement. But that doesn't mean everyone who works for the government is completely honest. A very wealthy prisoner can promise almost anything to a low level guard and get a response. Brenda got to someone who just walked out with her at the end of his shift and disappeared."

"So now what?" I asked.

"We've got a search going on. She'll turn up somewhere. A woman like that can't live without spending a lot of money. We've tapped accounts that she's likely to use and will be able to track the transactions. She's definitely gone from Belize but there's a lot of Caribbean to disappear into. We've sealed the borders to her under every known alias she has."

"That makes me feel so much better," I said. "Just a thought, Jordan, but she won't use any of the accounts you're watching. She probably has a million dollars-worth of ATM cards in her purse. And with ready cash, she could buy a birth certificate, citizenship, and a passport for someplace like Nicaragua or Ecuador."

"Thanks for the tip. We've shut down her base of operations. The Committee is hiding behind a cloak of respectability and would turn her in if she dared to contact one of them. They all know what thin ice they're walking on right now. They'd turn in their own mothers. They're all a little relieved Brenda is out of the picture."

"I'll be relieved when I know she's really out of it. I'll sleep better if you catch her."

"I'll do that. What are you doing for dinner tonight? Or should I make appointments with your assistant?"

"Um… Is this a business meeting?"

"It was more… well, no… I just thought… Well, I promised to take you to dinner as a thank you."

"Are you asking me out on a date?" I asked.

"Um… More like a fig."

"What?"

"It's between friends. Just dinner to catch up and thank you." My sigh was probably loud enough for Cinnamon to hear.

So, how do you dress for a fig?

{29}
Unexpected visitors

IT'S WAY PAST TIME to get back to my studies. I've moved. I have a new office. I have an assistant. I have no clients. Lars reminded me on Christmas that my thesis is due in just three weeks. It's almost done but I really have to focus these next two weeks. I'll have Cinnamon proofread this again when I've finished this time.

On retainer

ABOUT 10:30, CINNAMON knocked on my door and asked if I could take a visitor. I didn't even think about not doing it. I should probably consider having appointments instead of interruptions.

Angel walked in and closed the door behind her.

I'd never seen her like this. Her makeup is always perfect. She dresses perfectly. She's just so perfect all the time. But the Angel standing in my office didn't have any makeup on and it looked like she'd been crying.

"I look a wreck," she declared. "Deb, I *am* a wreck. I don't know what to do!" She burst into tears and I dredged up some motherly instinct from somewhere and hugged her. We sat on the sofa together and I dried her eyes with a tissue. God knows I've been doing enough crying the past month. I ought to know what to do about it. That's a myth, by the way. Doesn't help at all.

"What is it, Angel?" I asked. "I owe you my life. Please don't ever regret saving it." I just knew she was off on having shot Ray. She's never talked about it but I know it's on her mind. It's been on mine. We both know it's just something between the two of us. Neither of us will ever talk about it to anyone else.

"It's not that," she replied. "I don't regret for a minute what I did out there. I'd do it again right now. Faster this time."

"What is it then?"

"Simon." That said it all. You know, I have to admit, when I first heard about Angel and Simon I kind of kissed it off. Rich man. Golddigger. Get what you can and get out while you can. But when I saw them together in Croatia… I mean, the way he looked at her like she was the beginning and the end of the universe. And she was the happiest I'd ever seen a person when she was around him. Pull out all the clichés you want about old men and young women; these two were crazy in love.

"Tell me about it," I said.

"I got a message," she answered. "He's hiding and isn't coming out until he's sure Brenda is permanently out of the picture." Maybe I should have told Angel Brenda was on the loose again but it didn't cross my mind. I'm not sure if I could have told her even if it had. "He says until then, we'll have to live apart. It was such a beautiful love letter. But he didn't tell me where he's hiding so I can't run off and join him."

"You want me to track him down?" I asked apprehensively. So much for getting my thesis finished. But if Angel asked me to track down Simon, you know I'd do it.

"No. He's right. I'm thinking I should find a nice secluded retreat somewhere and disappear for a while. I wish I knew how to disguise myself and get a false identity like you do. That woman! She's a spiteful horrid bitch. She'll hurt me just to hurt Simon."

"I could be your mutual point of contact," I said, volunteering before I thought it through.

"I might need that if I decide to go. But that's not why I came."

"What's up?"

"Simon says give you a retainer." She was fishing in a purse the size of Lake Washington and I was sure she'd come out with a floppy salmon. Instead, she emerged with a little business card box. She handed it to me and I opened it. It was full of credit cards—the kind of ATM card she sells through her travel agency. There must have been, OMG! a hundred of them.

"There's a limit on how much I can put on an individual card and not draw attention," she explained. "$9,999.99. If I put $10,000 on one, someone comes to investigate. I could be liable for all kinds of civil and criminal penalties if I don't have every bit of paperwork in order. Your friend Jordan would arrest me. That's how we've always worked it. The guys come in and buy $10,000 minus a penny at a time and give me a $2,000 fee. It's pretty much like having a pocket full of $10,000 bills." She pulled a dollar bill out of her purse. "There's $999,999 on those cards. This makes it an even million." She handed me the dollar bill. "Simon says he wants a good detective on retainer, just in case he needs to be found again. He'll leave you a clue."

"Angel," I exclaimed. "I can't take this."

"Sure you can," she said. "Simon says. He's a good man, Deb. He knows a good detective has to be able to put her hands on cash at any time. This is invisible. Just put them in your private safe and pull them out when you need one. It never hits the books if you are careful. If you are extravagant and live beyond your means, the treasury will come down on you for tax evasion. If you keep it quiet, you'll always have a cushion. You're smart. You'll do what Simon says."

Angel stood up to leave. I didn't know what to say. Is that where the money Dag left me came from? The instructions were almost the same.

I'm twenty-seven years old. What have I gotten myself into?

"Cinnamon?" I called.

She came bouncing into my office and perched her cute little derriere on the edge of my new desk. *Damn.* I could hear Dag chuckling from far across the great divide.

"What's up, Sugar?" she said. I finally got it. As far as she was concerned, we were Cinnamon and Sugar.

"Here's a dollar," I said. "Fill out a retainer contract and receipt. Make it out in the name of Simon Barnett."

"You want me to take this to the bank?"

"No. Just staple it to the contract and file it."

"This is a strange business."

Secret keeper

I'D STUDIED MOST of the night, revising the conclusion of my thesis. It was much stronger now, but my eyes were scarcely open. And I had to make that call I'd been avoiding. Maizie tugged me along on the leash to Tovoni's and I felt much better after Jackie served me and gave Maizie her cookie. I just sat there inhaling the aroma. It woke my senses and I felt better even before I'd had a sip. When Maizie finished her cookie and got a drink of water, we waved goodbye and headed down to the office.

I pulled the card I'd received at the memorial service from my pocket and stared at it for five minutes before I finally made the call. I hoped she was awake. According to the information I had, she was shooting on location in Nassau. I was shocked when she answered her own phone.

"Miss Marx, this is Deb Riley in Seattle."

"Please, Deb. I thought we established that I'm just Cali."

"Thank you, Cali. I didn't want to disturb you earlier but you asked me to call about the plans for Dag's ashes." I heard a deep sigh. She didn't say anything, so I went on. "He asked to have them scattered on a beach up north of here. I feel like I've been negligent in fulfilling his wishes because of… well, I had to finish a job he asked me to do and it's eaten all my time this month. I think I should do it on New Year's Eve. I wanted to let you know."

"Thank you, Deb. It's the beach that's in that painting, isn't it? Shooting has shut down for the holiday and I've been doing nothing but sitting in my room reading. Can I call you back at this number when I know my travel plans?"

"You'll come?"

"Yeah. I loved Dag as the father I never knew. I'll definitely be there."

IT WAS A surprise to me that Cali Marx was coming home to Seattle for the scattering of Dag's ashes. I thought I was just making a courtesy call. I hoped she didn't want to stay with me. Or maybe I hoped she did.

Ack! Get back to it. The effect of *Johnson v. Palmyra*, 387 S.W.3d 683 (Tenn. App. 2008) on the receipt of evidence from anonymous sources in criminal prosecution. I printed a dozen pages and took them to Cinnamon to proofread as I attacked the next section.

About 3:00, she knocked on my door. I'd been shuffling pages back and forth all day and I assumed she had another batch to give me. She'd been asking questions about portions of the thesis and we were both getting into sharing insights. It was good practice for defending the paper in a few weeks. She slipped inside and closed the door.

"Miss Riley," she said. My head jerked up to see why she was so formal. "There is a Miss Horseshoe here to see you. At least I think that's her name. She's really nervous and has a very thick accent." It didn't sound familiar but I could use a break. I gathered my papers into a neat stack and set my laptop on top of it. Closed.

"Okay," I said. "Show her in."

Well, at least I wasn't dealing with another blonde. She had coal black hair and stood about five-one. Petite. Anxious. She looked around furtively and finally faced me. She was beautiful.

"Are you Miss Deborah Riley," she asked with a Scandinavian accent so thick I was tempted to call the Swedish American Center to get an interpreter.

"Yes," I said. She rummaged in her purse and produced a letter that she put on the desk in front of me. Now I knew who she was. Teresia Hjortschoe. I had no idea how it was pronounced. I sent the letter to her at Dag's request when he died.

"Did you read this?" she demanded. God, I'd thought about it. Miss Nosy Pants.

"No," I said. "Dag left me a letter asking me to send this to you after he died. I'm so sorry for the loss of your cousin, Miss Hjortshoe." That did it. I had an ocean being cried in my office again. Please stop, I thought. I can't take any more of this. If I let it come out again, I might never stop crying. I led her to the sofa and offered her a tissue from my unending supply. I better tell Cinnamon this box is running low. She pulled herself together.

"I'm sorry," she said. "Dag was my favorite cousin. He's always been there for me."

"I didn't know," I said. "Losing Dag was hard on all of us but it must be devastating for you."

"Did Dag tell you about his trip to Sweden last fall?"

"I was here, holding down the fort, so to speak. He was very disappointed he didn't make it in time to see his aunt before she died. Having two losses in such a short time must have been very hard on your family."

"Cousin Dag saved my life," she said flatly. Dag hadn't told me about that. In fact, the first I'd heard of a cousin Teresia was when I was instructed to send the letter. We talked for quite a while and I pointed out the view of the ferries leaving dock that Dag loved so much. She wanted to know about what I was doing behind his desk and how I planned to continue the business being 'so young.' She even asked about the business name, D.H. Investigations. Well, I'm Deborah H. Riley, so I've decided to keep the company name as is. I had the impression, once she settled down, that she was interviewing me, trying to find out what kind of person I am. She never got around to telling me exactly how Dag saved her life. We'd talked for nearly an hour when she pointed at the letter still lying on my desk.

"Please keep this in your safe place for me," she said. "Cousin Dag kept it as surety for my good behavior. His requirement of me was he would send this to authorities if I was ever accused of a criminal offense. It will guarantee I am convicted. Will you keep it safe against the same end?"

Damn! Heavy stuff. I looked at the envelope. As far as I could tell, it was the same one I'd tucked in a mailer with the letter about Dag's death—still unopened. I just knew I was going to regret this for the next God knows how many years. I put the envelope in my pencil drawer. As soon as she leaves, I thought, I'll put it in the vault.

"As Dag's partner and friend," I said, "I will keep this just like he did. I will not look at its contents and will only forward it to appropriate authorities if I hear you are accused of a major crime." I used her words as closely as I could remember them so there was no room for misunderstanding. I've just become some kind of secret keeper. Where will it end?

I'll take Teresia and Cinnamon to dinner tonight and explain the plans for scattering Dag's ashes on New Year's Eve. Just two days away. I'm glad Teresia showed up when she did.

—————— +―+―+―+―++||||||||++―+―+―+― ——————

Into the nightmare—again

MAYBE IT WAS having someone near who was so close to Dag in a life I knew nothing about. Maybe it was the crash from all the adrenalin I'd burned this month. Maybe because I was sleeping with Maizie in Dag's apartment in Dag's bed. Maybe it's because I'm just a bad person and they are punishment for my sins. Whatever. The nightmares were back.

———+—+++++++++++++———

I SAT IN my chair, unable to move, tied by unseen bonds. I held my eyes tightly closed so I couldn't see them. The ghosts of my mother and father, the taunting children in my school, the refrigerator-like Oksamma and his sidekick Bradley. Maybe Ray Hawkins would join them to taunt me from his watery grave. They would laugh at me. Call me Freak, Bozo, Baldy. They would tear out my hair by the fistful and throw it in my face. They would laugh as I cried out to stop. If I opened my eyes, it would all be there in front of me.

I forced them shut. I screamed that I wouldn't look, but inevitably my eyes were pried open and I looked around me in the dreamworld I had created. It was worse. The dead were all there—even Dag. But they were silent. They stared at me and waited.

"What? What!" I wailed. "What do you want? Just do your worst. Stop staring at me!" I looked pleadingly at Dag but his image dissolved and his cousin Teresia was staring at me instead. The dead all faded, only to be replaced by the living. Simon, Angel, Lars. They were joined by everyone I knew. Mrs. Prior, Jordan, Cinnamon, Geoff, Teri, even Davy. The dead had all been replaced by the living—except Dag was back among them. He still stood there staring at me in silence.

"What? What!" I screamed again. "What do you want?"

"You have it all," Dag whispered as he gently touched my bald head and comforted me. "You have friends, money, trust, power. You have it all. Now what kind of person are you going to be?"

They all just stood there looking at me. All asking. What kind of person am I going to be?

I was awake now, rigid in my bed. Even awake within the dim light of Dag's apartment, I could see them. When I closed my eyes, they became more real. The tears flowed. It was worse.

It was so much worse.

{30}
Kidnapped

FINALLY SATURDAY! I promised myself I would sleep in as long as I wanted. I would go out to play with Maizie, go to the park, have coffee at Tovoni's. Then I'd pick up Teresia at her hotel and we'd have an elegant lunch overlooking the Sound and talk about plans for scattering Dag's ashes tomorrow. We'd share stories and have a cry and I'd make a new friend.

Call for backup

"WE'RE GOING OUT to play, Mrs. Prior," I said. "I was wearing jeans and a punk band T-shirt I'd found among Dag's clothes. And my winter coat. It sure wasn't warm enough to go without that.

"Have a nice day at the office, dear," she answered.

"No office today. We're going to the park and play. Then maybe we'll get all prettied up and I'll take Maizie to meet Dag's cousin."

"Really?" Mrs. Prior knelt down and Maizie danced on her hind legs to kiss her. "Maizie thinks you should go to the office. She says she has unfinished business there. After coffee."

"Maizie? This is supposed to be a fun day for the two of us. You really want to go to the office?" I said. Her little front legs were beating the air while she danced on her hinds. "You know what that means? I need to change clothes." One thing Dag had always insisted on was professional wear in the office. I know. It's my office now. I can dress however I want. I went upstairs and changed from ripped jeans into a pair of wool slacks and a sweater. Casual Saturday. Or as Dag would say, 'Weekends and holidays are days I don't wear a tie to the office.'

We stopped at Tovoni's and I had my espresso while Maizie primly lay beside me nibbling on her biscuit. Then we headed down the hill. We were almost to the office when my phone rang. I glanced at the screen wondering what Cinnamon was doing awake at this hour. It wasn't even ten yet!

"Hey, sexy," I said. "What's the good word?"

"Um… Miss Riley?" Cinnamon's voice sounded hesitant and very un-Cinnamon.

"What is it Cinnamon?" I asked.

"Miss Riley, I'm in trouble," she said formally.

"Where are you, Cinnamon? Are you in jail?"

"No. I'm at the Condo."

"I thought it was closed up."

"Ms. B has a key." *Damn!* Brenda Lamb Barnett was back in town? "She says you are to come directly to the Condo. If you send for police, she'll take me off the roof with her. I'm sorry, Deb. I'm scared." The line went abruptly dead. Cinnamon must be scared. Her voice sounded wooden. Or maybe she was trying to tell me something else. Was I going to have to face down Davy? Did she have other goons with her?

I jogged the rest of the way to the office with Maizie. Ms. B isn't the only one with a key to the Condo. I glanced up from the window and could see the rooftop garden. *Hang in there, Cinnamon. Help is on the way.*

I'd been through this before. Dag and I went through every move when he rescued me from the Condo and analyzed what went wrong and what went right. The one thing I learned was to call for backup. I dialed Jordan's number.

"She's unbalanced," I said, "so it's possibly a credible threat. I can't imagine that Cinnamon couldn't fight her off if they were alone. There must be someone else with her."

"Put on a wire and give me the frequency, Deb. I'll let you take point so we don't spook her but I'll be right behind you. It's time to close this down once and for all."

That was comforting. I opened the vault and grabbed one of the little transmitters Dag had collected. I need to replenish the stock of electronics. I'm going through things kind of fast.

I looked at Maizie and she barked. Yeah. This time I'm taking reinforcements in with me.

"Let's go, partner," I said.

———|—|—|—|-||||||||||-|—|—|—|———

Gunpoint

MAIZIE AND I walked through the front door of the building like we owned the place. I used my keycard to access the elevator and went straight to the Condo. There was no sense climbing stairs or using a service elevator. I was expected and was sure Brenda was watching me. As soon as we were in the elevator, I unsnapped Maizie's leash. "Keep a low profile, girl," I said. It was kind of funny. She's only eight inches tall.

The elevator doors opened and I stepped into the entryway. Crime scene tape was still stretched across the metal detector and I could see the device wasn't lit up. I just ripped through the tape and marched straight to the office. I didn't bother to knock. She was watching and I was on my way. I lost track of where Maizie was but didn't see anyone else in the Condo. I keyed in my security code and pushed the door open, dropping my bag in the doorway to block it open.

What I saw wasn't what I expected. Brenda and Cinnamon were there, all right. Cinnamon was tied in the very chair I'd spent time in a month ago. It looked like she could have gotten free if she tried. Brenda was tied to the desk chair with tape across her mouth. Behind her, Angel held a gun.

"Angel?"

"I knew you'd want to be here for this," she said. "We'll never be free until she's dead. She blamed Dag for killing Simon and she's made it impossible for us to be together as long as she's alive. We're just going to arrange a little accident."

"Angel, you can't do this," I said. "Let's just call the police and turn her over."

"What good are they?" she demanded. "They let her loose when they had her in jail. They couldn't keep her confined in Belize. Oh, yes. I knew where she was all along. And I knew she was back in town." She threw a cash card on the desk. "Don't ever believe you can't be traced through these. I own the database. I tagged all the cards I knew she had and watched for the account to activate. When she showed up in Seattle, I was waiting. This is where it started and this is where it ends."

Angel looked a mess. Her hair was ratted and mascara was smeared. Her clothes looked like she'd slept in them. She had a wild crazy look in her eyes and the gun trembled as she held it on Brenda.

"Angel, bad as she is and as much as she deserves to die, we can't just execute her."

"We're not. We're rescuing poor Cinnamon. Ms. B was trying to throw her off the roof. Didn't you get the message? We came to rescue our dear friend. Just like I saved Simon when Ray tried to kill him. She'll just tip over the edge of the roof." Angel looked worse with every word she spoke, her mouth pulled back in a grimace. Her clothes were too tight. She looked old. She was turning into what she hated right in front of us. She looked like Brenda. Insane. *Now what am I going to do?*

"Let's talk this out," I said. "Let's hear what she has to say." Brenda kept shaking her head frantically.

"No! I've heard enough of her. Let's go." Angel waved the gun around and gave Brenda a push out of the chair. She stumbled to a knee and stood up. "Bring Cinnamon," Angel snapped at me. I moved behind my assistant and untied her hands. She looked fearful and I removed her gag.

"I'm sorry, Deb. I thought we were just going to hold her for the police. I didn't know what Angel planned. Honest, I'm sorry." I hushed her by laying a finger on her lips.

"Just follow my lead. Help is on the way." We followed Angel and Brenda out of the office and through the poolroom to the roof. "Maizie," I whispered. My little buddy popped her head around the corner and followed us out.

When we were all standing in the frigid wind, Angel pushed Brenda toward the edge of the roof.

"You can't just toss her over with her hands tied and her mouth taped shut," I said calmly. "It doesn't look like either an accident or suicide."

"Cinnamon," Angel barked. "Go untie her." Cinnamon obediently went to Brenda and first ripped the tape off her mouth. If the old woman was growing any lip whiskers, they were waxed as she screamed and started a steady stream of invective.

"You stupid bitches!" she yelled. "You'll never get away with this. I own your whore asses. You'll all hang. Three blonde cunts dangling from adjoining ropes. I will be there to watch."

Cinnamon worked the knot loose from Brenda's hands, paying more attention to Angel's gun than to what she was doing. I saw it a moment too late to act. As soon as Brenda's hands were free, she wrapped an arm around Cinnamon and pulled her in front as a shield. Cinnamon screamed and struggled but she's really tiny and was no match for Brenda. And they were dangerously close to the low wall at the edge of the roof.

"Now get back!" Brenda yelled, propelling Cinnamon in front of her toward the door. "If I go over the edge, so does she."

"You see," Angel snarled coldly. "I told you she was threatening to pull Cinnamon over the edge with her. Now I'll have to shoot her." Angel raised the gun to take careful aim with her shaking hands. There was no way she could make the shot with Brenda ducking behind Cinnamon but I could see she was going to shoot anyway.

I saw Maizie streak across the roof from the open door Brenda was moving toward and went into action. I grabbed Angel's arm and forced it up as she fired. She swung toward me and I used her momentum to trip her and wrench the gun from her hand. It went flying across the roof and Angel went down on one knee. In the meantime, Maizie had run up behind Brenda and bit her on the calf. Brenda fell backward with Cinnamon on top of her but didn't let go. Maizie ran in a circle barking and went for Brenda's arm. It loosened enough for Cinnamon to roll free but Angel was on her feet and diving on top of Brenda.

There was no way to get between the two women, each of whom was bent on killing the other. They grappled to their feet in a catfight, pulling hair and scratching at each other. Angel had one hand in a chokehold. Maizie circled, diving in to nip where she thought it would help. I reached to grab Angel's hand away from Brenda's throat. When I loosened her grip, Brenda drove her elbow into Angel's face, knocking her out of my grip and into the low wall. She teetered there for a moment and I thought she had regained her balance as I reached a hand for her. But Brenda rushed her to give her that last push over the edge. Angel caught Brenda in a hug as she passed the point of no return and both women disappeared over the edge of the roof. I rushed to look and sat back on my butt. Cinnamon wrapped her arms around me and rocked me back and forth.

I could hear voices in the Condo behind us. Maizie crawled into my lap as officers came through the door onto the roof. There was nothing left for them to do. Jordan hobbled through the Condo before he heard the report of two women going over the edge. He rushed out to find us as quickly as he could with a cane and cast on his leg. Cinnamon abandoned me and rushed into his arms. I didn't blame her. If my legs had any bones in them, I'd join her.

Two officers approached me but kept their distance as Maizie growled every time they got near. They looked to Jordan for instructions and he motioned them away.

"Secure the apartment," he commanded. "I'll take it from here. Have an ambulance standing by. She's in shock." I think that's what he said. It might as well have been, "Get a net. I'm throwing her off the roof." He managed to get down on one knee with his cast sticking out. He let Maizie sniff the back of his hand and she butted it to get her ears scratched.

"That's a good girl, Maizie," he said. "You did a good job protecting Riley. Let's take care of her now. It's been a hard day."

Cinnamon helped us to our feet and reached out to gently straighten my wig. We both leaned on him as we made our way back to the elevator. *Who was supporting whom?* Jordan shook Maizie's leash at the door and she sat waiting to be hooked up.

EMTs helped Cinnamon and me into the ambulance and we clung to each other as they checked our vitals. Jordan and Maizie sat across from us waiting for them to finish their exam.

I would be happy if I never saw the inside of an ambulance or a hospital again.

I would be happy if I never saw someone die again.

I would be happy if I never lost another friend.

I would be happy. But I'm not.

{31}
Sail away

M Y PHONE CHIMED about the time I finished making my statement. It had taken about two hours before I felt like I could talk but they discharged me from the hospital into Jordan's care with Cinnamon beside me. Everything had been recorded from the wire I wore, so I was able to fill in the visual record as the voices replayed in my ears.

A wake

"THIS IS DEB RILEY," I said when I answered the line.

"Deb, it's Cali Marx. I just got in. Can we meet for dinner?"

"Cali, I'm so glad you're here. It's been a terrible day. I… Um… Dag's cousin Teresia is here, too. Do you mind having a few more people?"

"That would be fine. Let's cap it at ten. The concierge here says he can get us a table at Trace for seven o'clock. That's in the W Hotel. And don't worry about the cost. It's my little contribution to the memory of my dad. Okay?"

"Great. Thank you for calling, Cali. You're a bright spot in a dark day. See you at seven."

It took no time for Jordan and Cinnamon to agree to dinner. I'd already made arrangements to pick up Teresia, who was staying at a much less expensive hotel downtown. I called Teri and she said she was with Geoff watching his team play in Orlando. I didn't know who else to invite, but on the spur of the moment I asked Mrs. Prior and Lars if they'd join us.

———————————————

FOR HAVING SUCH a somber occasion, our dinner was still lively. Cali was a popular young actress and a few people came up to ask for an autograph or photo until the Maitre d' simply stationed a waiter near us to direct people away. And then we were all telling stories of how we met Dag, what he'd done for us, and how we'd miss him.

Cali told about her mother falling in love with Dag and how they'd planned to get married. The story of the night Cali was kidnapped and her mother died was heartrending but also endearing as Cali said Dag had never missed a premiere of a movie she was in or even opening night of a play.

Jordan knew Cali from 'the old days.' He told about how he'd arrested Dag in order to get him out of the office with all the backup disks for the fraud he was investigating. He said that a few years ago they'd worked together to stop the world's greatest hacker from starting World War III.

Teresia mentioned he'd been through Sweden with his mother a few years ago and was very mysterious about where he was traveling. She'd helped him dye his blonde hair before he left for an adventure in Asia that brought him back three weeks later looking sick and tired. A few days with the family, though, and he'd taken his mother back to Seattle. Jordan nodded and confirmed Dag had erased himself in order to make that trip.

Cinnamon, of course, had a story about how she'd attempted to seduce Dag and when she found out he was with me, had decided on a threesome that never quite materialized.

Lars talked about commanding Dag in the Navy and then waiting for him to show up in class at the college.

I told about tailing him in Las Vegas for three days and having to intentionally blow my cover so he'd discover me. It was also my first introduction to his heart condition as he had an attack that evening.

In all, we talked and laughed all evening and then said our goodbyes. It would be an early morning.

———————————————

Goodbye, dear friend

PEOPLE STARTED ARRIVING at my apartment at eight o'clock Sunday morning, New Year's Eve. Teresia and Cali shared a cab from downtown and seemed like they were becoming fast friends. Teresia had heard Dag mention Cali on numerous occasions. I wondered why he'd never told me about her.

Dag's high school girlfriend, Rhonda—the one who painted the seascape he loved—showed up just a few minutes before Lars Andersen. Mrs. Prior brought a batch of cinnamon rolls she'd baked that morning—thanks to Pillsbury. Jackie, the barista at Tovoni's, saved the day by bringing enough coffee for everyone and somehow having the perfect drink for each of us. And a cookie for Maizie.

I know there were others I should have invited. When Cinnamon and Jordan arrived, though, we were ready to go. Rhonda knew the exact spot. She'd painted it forty some years ago. I realized the only person in this room I knew six months ago was Lars Andersen, my thesis advisor. How things changed. It was like I'd suddenly entered a new solar system and a new sun is shining and new stars are in the night sky. I don't know if I'll ever get used to it.

We loaded the cars—including Dag's ashes and Maizie—and started the parade to the north end of Whidbey Island near Deception Pass.

———— +-+-+-+-++‖‖+++-+-+ ————

IT WAS AWKWARD at times. There were no dry eyes. Hell, I could hardly see to drive up there. The sky was overcast but once we got off the Mukilteo Ferry on Whidbey Island, Teresia and I put the top down on the Mustang. It was just over forty degrees out but we cranked up the heater to the max and the volume on the radio. Maizie joined our singing with occasional howls.

Once we were parked, Rhonda showed us how to get down to the beach.

It was beautiful. I recognized it immediately, even though I'd only seen it in Rhonda's painting. We walked down the path with Lars and Cinnamon helping Jordan. When the path opened out onto the beach, we all stopped short. A man stood by the edge of the water, wearing a winter coat with a hat pulled down over his ears. We followed his eyes as they gazed out across the endless expanse of the Strait of Juan de Fuca to the open sea. While we silently watched, he turned and walked away toward the south. A black lab came running up to him and he threw a stick farther down the beach. The lab chased it and we watched until he was out of sight.

We walked slowly across the sand to the edge of the water and all stood where the man had been, looking out across the water.

None of us knew what to do. I held the urn cradled in my arms like a baby. We came here to say goodbye and all we could do was stand there silently looking out to sea for about fifteen minutes as each person made their way to touch the urn and then retreat. It was too bad none of us were particularly religious. We should have had some parting words to say. We should have said, "Sail away, old friend." We should have said we loved him—there would never be anyone like him in this world. We should have said we'd see him in the next life. Or that I'd be worthy of the gift he'd given me.

But it was all silent until I knelt and unscrewed the cap on the urn. Then everyone just silently stepped away. They stepped back and left me there alone with Dag and Maizie. I stood up with the urn outstretched in my hands and started to slowly let the ashes fall.

I don't know what suddenly gripped me—if it was Maizie's bark or the sudden gust of wind—but the next thing I knew, I was spinning madly in a circle with the urn outstretched and ashes scattering in every direction and the wind picking them up in a huge cloud around me and Maizie jumping and snapping and barking like crazy.

When I finally stopped spinning, the urn was empty. The ashes had not yet settled but the wind was blowing them farther out on the water in a cloud. Everyone closed in around me and we all put our arms around each other and cried and waved at the cloud and said goodbye and I love you.

WE STOPPED FOR a late lunch at a little diner in Edmonds, just so we didn't have to part yet. We laughed at each other and set the empty urn on the table in a place of honor. We probably looked pretty weird to the staff and any passers-by. But we didn't care.

It was finally time to go. Lars had agreed to take Teresia and Cali to the airport. The two women pulled me aside.

"Thank you, Deb Riley," Teresia said formally. "I loved my cousin. In addition to everything else, he was a faithful guardian of my secrets. I am so glad he had you and that I can trust you with those same secrets."

"Teresia," I answered, "I don't know what your secrets are, but they'll be safe in the vault. I loved Dag, too, and even if I didn't do it for you, I'd do it for his sake."

"The same goes for me," Cali said. "I had Dag do some investigative research for me about ten years ago. It was just before my mother died. I find I am still not ready to learn what he discovered. Perhaps when I marry and have children of my own, I'll be ready to collect that research from you."

"It is safe in my keeping, Cali. I'm so glad I met you and discovered Dag's family. If ever I can do anything else for either of you, please don't hesitate to call me. Thank you both for coming to see Dag off with us."

"You have some strange customs," Teresia laughed, "but it seemed like just the kind of thing he would do. I hope I'll see you again sometime."

HOME IN MY pajamas, I held Maizie in my lap as I looked up at the painting. I'd decided to keep it hanging in the same place Dag had it and curled up in the recliner with our dog. I'd selected a CD at random from Dag's collection and soothing tones were playing through the speakers.

I just heard a soft knock at my door. Someone has decided not to leave me alone on New Year's Eve. I'm betting it's Jordan.

Of course, it could be Cinnamon.

Or both.

You know what? Either way, I'm going to get kissed at midnight tonight.

The End

www.ingramcontent.com/pod-product-compliance
Lightning Source LLC
Chambersburg PA
CBHW051256250626
47155CB00009B/3313